◆ BOOK TWO ◆

GRAIL QUEST

MORGAIN'S REVENGE

LAURA ANNE GILMAN

HARPERCOLLINS*PUBLISHERS*
A PARACHUTE PRESS BOOK

Library of Congress Cataloging-in-Publication Data

Gilman, Laura Anne.

Morgain's revenge / Laura Anne Gilman.— 1st ed.

p. cm. — (Grail quest ; 2)

"A Parachute Press Book."

Summary: The Quest for the Holy Grail is postponed again when Ailis
is kidnapped by Morgain the sorceress, and her friends, Newt and Gerard,
must leave the court of King Arthur seeking to rescue her, accompanied by
a grumbling knight.

ISBN-10: 0-06-077282-4 (trade bdg.) — ISBN-13: 978-0-06-077282-6 (trade bdg.)

ISBN-10: 0-06-077283-2 (lib. bdg.) — ISBN-13: 978-0-06-077283-3 (lib. bdg.)

[1. Magic—Fiction. 2. Knights and knighthood—Fiction. 3. Morgan le Fay
(Legendary character)—Fiction. 4. Merlin (Legendary character)—Fiction.
5. Arthur, King—Fiction. 6. Middle Ages—Fiction. 7. Great Britain—
History—To 1066—Fiction.] I. Title. II. Series.

PZ7.G43325Mor 2006   2005021106

[Fic]—dc22   CIP

                                                              AC

1 2 3 4 5 6 7 8 9 10

❖

First Edition

For CGAG,
who came through when needed

ONE

The sunlight filtered down through the large window that dominated the room at the top of the Queen's Tower; its glass was the clearest and finest that craftsmen could make. Only the best was offered to the Queen of Camelot, Guinevere, and her court.

Today that court, fifteen ladies-in-waiting, chosen for their good breeding, fine manners, and gracious speech, was scattered about the room, sitting on cushioned benches or padded chairs pushed together for better gossiping. They worked at their stitchery and listened to a musician playing a lute quietly off in the corner. The queen sat in the center of the solar on a simple high-backed wooden chair that was practically hidden by the long purple folds of her skirt. Two maids held up brocaded fabrics for her consideration, while a master craftsman stood off to one side, awaiting her decision.

"Oh, dear. Allison, *what* have you been thinking to let your threads become so . . . tangled?"

The woman speaking to her was Caitrin. The eldest daughter of one of the queen's cousins, she was sweet-faced—but with the soul of a viper and a tongue as poisonous.

Ailis, still not used to the unfamiliar twist on her name that the ladies-in-waiting had given her, looked up from her embroidery. The soft, blue thread had indeed become less a field of flowers than a mess of knots in the fabric she was working on. A woman sitting on the chair nearest to her giggled, then hid her smile behind one hand and looked away when Ailis glared at her.

Ailis suppressed her instinctive response to Caitrin's usual cruelty, and merely bent her head back down to her work. *Calm. Be calm.* She hadn't asked to be lifted from the life of a servant, any more than she had asked to become a servant in the first place. She had little to say in her own affairs since her parents had died in a battle in the early years of Arthur's reign. But when she and her friends, Newt and Gerard, had broken the sleep-spell cast by the sorceress Morgain, the queen had decided that Ailis deserved a better future. Gerard, a squire, had also been rewarded. He was given the opportunity to ride out with the great Quest to find the Holy Grail—the very Quest that Morgain's spell had been designed to prevent.

But they never asked me what I wanted, she thought, many times since she had been sent here.

Being taught needlework, or how to read out loud in a properly modulated voice, wasn't such a bad thing. It was certainly better than carrying pitchers and platters, which had been her place before. And serving at her queen's side was better than scrubbing floors, which would have been her fate had she been born to a servant's life, rather than coming to it as an orphaned child. But no matter how nice the surroundings, how light the work, the truth was that she had less freedom now than ever before.

Only Newt, safe in the stable with his beloved horses, had avoided having his life turned completely upside down. Some days Ailis thought that he had been the more fortunate one.

Ailis looked around the room, careful not to make eye contact with Lady Caitrin, who was still lurking like a vulture waiting to pluck some reaction from her victim. In truth, some of the ladies-in-waiting

3

who served the queen had made Ailis's new life almost enjoyable, calling her "pet" and making a fuss over her the way she thought her mother might have, if her mother had lived.

But then there were the ladies like Caitrin, who thought she was still nothing more than a serving girl with too many liberties. *They never asked me what I wanted,* she thought again, but refused to let the sigh she felt building inside her find release. It would be ungrateful, ill-bred. It would prove Caitrin right. Besides, what *did* she want? Ailis didn't know . . . exactly.

With a soft whisper of skirts, one of the women gently nudged Ailis over on her bench and sat down beside her. "Here. Let me help."

Ailis handed her stitchery over to Lady Roslyn with relief. The older girl had come with Lady Guinevere's entourage when Guinevere had married Arthur. She had always been kind, even when Ailis was merely a serving girl.

"Ah." Roslyn nodded sagely, handing the needlework back. "You're pulling too hard when you come back up through the fabric. Sweetness, don't let Caitrin worry at you. You'll find the manner of it, soon enough."

Ailis didn't want to find the manner of it—not of embroidery and not of the company of these women. *Maybe,* she thought. *Maybe Caitrin* was *right.* There were days when Ailis felt like she needed to run, screaming, back to the servants' quarters where she didn't feel quite so vulnerable, so very much a target, so dratted restless. She wanted to be out of the sweetly scented, sunlight-filled chamber, with its comfortable cushions and young minstrels, and its inhabitants—friendly and otherwise.

She was suffocating, unable to breathe in her pretty new dress, her hair now tied up under a simple veil that wrapped modestly around her neck instead of her former long russet braid hanging free over her shoulder.

Just that morning, the queen had spoken of setting Ailis up with a suitable match; nothing too high for her comfort, but a marriage where she would be the mistress of her own home. She would be matched with a good-stock knight perhaps; a man who could make much of himself and his name with hard work and skill.

Ailis knew she should be grateful. And she was. But something inside her was dying every day she sat with these women, listening to them gossip. Weeks ago she had ridden on a magical race against time that led her across England in order to save her king. She had worn boy's trousers under her skirt for ease of movement, and matched verbal wits with Merlin, the greatest enchanter ever. She had bargained with bandits, and even faced down Morgain Le Fay, the king's sorceress half-sister. Ailis still had nightmares about that—horrible dreams in which rather than discovering the secret to Morgain's spell-casting, rather than escaping the sorceress's otherworld home on the Isle of Apples, she and Gerard and Newt had been caught by magic and locked forever in a windowless, doorless cell made of stone.

They had gotten lucky. No matter how often Merlin might say that luck was merely the stars aligning themselves with one's own preparedness, Ailis knew: They had gotten lucky.

Her luck ended there, though.

From that fateful moment when Morgain's spell had put every adult in Camelot into a dreamless sleep, everything in Ailis's life had changed. *She* had changed. And now Ailis needed more than days spent in a protected solar, no matter how easeful. She needed air. And she needed to find out what was going on in the rest of the castle! The great Quest for the Holy Grail had been postponed, after Morgain's sleep-spell ended. At the last contact she had had with Gerard, he told her and Newt that the Quest would be leaving Camelot soon—as soon as the Knights of the Round Table settled who would participate, and who would stay to protect the castle. He was still to go, although he did not know with which knights, or where he might be sent.

Ailis had been locked up with the ladies since then, and she couldn't discover anything more from the same giggly gossip, which never mentioned specifics, much less the fate of one specific lowly squire. It was driving her mad, not knowing what was happening with Gerard or with Newt. They had all gotten so close, only to be broken apart so easily— it hurt. Even more so because she didn't know if *they* were thinking or worrying about her at all.

"Ah, bother." A petulant voice broke into her thoughts. "I'm out of linen thread."

"I'll go fetch more," Ailis said, happy at the chance to go for a walk. Her shoulders tensed, wanting so badly to be out of there. But she smiled sweetly, projecting an intentional, innocent eagerness to please that had Lady Sharyn smiling back at her.

"Thank you, my dear. Gracelan, the chatelaine,

has a packet set aside for me of this particular color." It was a soft green, the color of new leaves in spring. The thread must have cost a fortune, which was why it was kept under the castle housekeeper's key.

"If it please my lady, I'll go now," Ailis said, slipping from her cushion near the queen's chair. She paused long enough to make a curtsey to Queen Guinevere, who looked up from her consultation with a dressmaker and nodded her absentminded permission for the girl to leave.

"Thank you, your grace," she said, dropping another curtsey and hurrying as quickly as she could across the wooden floor of the solar, while still taking approved ladylike steps. Her steps had never been very long, especially compared to the great lengths Newt and Gerard could cover, but now she was supposed to go even more slowly. "A lady must never walk, but glide," the dance instructor had told her and the other girls new to Guinevere's service. "Glide as you move. Do not swing your arms, but hold them gently at your sides, and glide."

She was a person, not a swan, for the pity of heaven! People *walked*. People even occasionally ran. But not ladies. Never ladies.

"Bah," she said under her breath, not loud enough

for anyone to hear. Ladies did not say "bah," either.

As the solar was up high in the Queen's Tower, it caught the sunlight all day. The stairway down to the main level was a circular thing cut out of stone, with steps more shallow than elsewhere. It might simply have been sized small, for a woman's foot, but something, some twitch of intuition honed by her earlier adventures, told Ailis there was more to it than that.

The narrow width and the shallow steps would make it nigh impossible for a man in armor to climb these stairs. And if such a man were to make it this far, he would have no room in which to swing his sword or draw a bow.

Thoughts like these made Ailis so uncomfortable in the company of the ladies-in-waiting. Not only did she know a world beyond the pampered, cushioned solar, but she knew what lay beyond the harder, but still sheltered, life of a castle servant.

Ailis was different. And she noticed things. Things gently bred, gently raised ladies were not meant to notice. Not to mention the fact that, sometimes, a voice sounded in the depths of her head, giving her advice and leading her to conclusions a simple serving girl might not otherwise reach. That had been why she had followed Gerard and Newt when they set off to find Merlin to lift the sleep-spell. She had heard that voice in her head, that voice that gave advice and pointed the way to answers; the voice that sounded much like Merlin the Enchanter. Even though Merlin never said anything to her directly to confirm that he had been the one speaking to her, who else could it have been?

But since the time the three had broken the spell and returned Arthur and his court to wakefulness, that voice had been painfully absent from her life. It might be because Merlin was simply preoccupied, trying to escape from the house of ice they had been forced to leave him in, trapped by his former student Nimue. Or perhaps he had tired of Ailis. Perhaps he had decided that the queen's favor and a well-placed marriage was the highest Ailis should aspire to, and she did not need the aid of an enchanter for that.

In truth, Ailis wasn't sure how she felt about marriage. Or enchanters. She did not know what she wanted out of life. She wasn't sure how she felt about anything anymore, except that she wanted more than what the queen's court was offering her.

No small amount of that dissatisfaction came from the fact that, when the trio had confronted

Morgain, the sorceress had called Ailis a witch-child. A witch! Her?

Magic was unnatural, for all that it was useful. It was fine for Merlin, who *was* magic, a creature of the Old Gods, the ones who had ruled these lands before the Romans came. He might serve Arthur, a Christian king, now, but his allegiances were to the fairy world. Ailis, on the other hand, was a mortal, a God-fearing mortal who valued her soul as it was. The thought of magic having anything to do with *her* was an uneasy one. It made people look at you strangely. Or step back in fear. Or call you names.

At the same time, she missed hearing Merlin's voice in the back of her head. She missed the warm glow she felt simply being around the talismans the three friends had collected on their quest. She missed feeling special.

"Want what you can't have, can't have what you want. You are a thankless child, Ailis, you are," she told herself, in a very poor imitation of Caitrin's voice. Then she looked around guiltily, although there was no way anyone could have heard her.

Having reached the bottom of the circular stairwell, Ailis started down the main hallway, then hesitated in her ladylike steps. It would take her forever, walking so sedately through the main halls.

Looking around, she noted only a few servants, none of them familiar to her, and one page, who gave a cheeky smile as he dashed past on some errand or another. Reaching up to tug at her hair, forgetting for a moment that it was no longer hanging freely over her shoulder, she came to a decision. Picking up the hem of her skirts in one hand so she could move more easily, she turned left into the smaller side-hallway the page had come out from, and took that, instead of the main corridor.

Walking with her own natural stride, Ailis could cover the distance in far less time. The secondary halls were servants' territory. Anyone who saw her here would be unlikely to reprimand her for moving in such an unseemly manner, or—worse yet—carry accusatory tales back to the solar. It felt like freedom, as much as she might expect to find, for at least a short time.

"And if I'm lucky, maybe I'll see someone who can tell me what's been going on!" Her voice carried farther in the stone hallway than she had expected. She jumped a little at the echo, then giggled at herself. Such a brave warrior she was, startled at her own voice!

She tried to mimic Newt's rangier style of walking as best she could, pulling the memory of it from her mind with surprising ease. He tilted forward a little, like so, and kept his hands in his pockets. She had no pockets in her skirt, of course, but she fisted her hands at her sides and bent at the elbows, just as he did. Odd that she could remember his walk so clearly when his face was a blur of raggedly cut hair and dark eyes in an otherwise unremarkable structure.

Turning the corner, Ailis could feel her spirits begin to rise. Yes, at this pace, she could finish this errand and still have time to stop by the stables to see if Newt had a few moments to talk. At least she knew where to find him. Gerard could be anywhere. She could hardly expect to just bump into him in the hallway, considering how large Camelot was, and how busy all the squires probably were. *No, seeing Gerard in the hallway would be as unlikely as finding the king himself here,* she thought.

She rounded another corner and almost without thinking, pulled herself back out of sight. Even as her spine hit the stone wall, her mind was trying to figure out what she had seen—and why she had reacted that way.

She closed her eyes and shook her head, but the

image remained. Had she hit her head at some point—was she hallucinating? No, it seemed unlikely. But so too was what she thought she had seen.

Praying that nobody would come up behind her unexpectedly, Ailis peeked cautiously around the corner, so that only the tip of her face showed. She had seen what she thought she had seen, indeed. A dark green glow, man-high and just as wide. Impossible. Incredible. *Magical.* And in the middle of it, likely creating it . . .

A cold sweat formed and dripped down Ailis's neck, running in a line down her spine. "Morgain? Here? In the *castle*?"

TWO

"And so, sire, I must protest at this plan, even as I understand why my fellow knights might think it needful . . ."

Gerard was standing against a wall with the other squires, each standing attendance to their master. A tapestry on the wall across the room's grand table showed a scene from Arthur's coronation: Arthur standing in front of the masses, Excalibur in his hand, Merlin off to his right and Sir Kay and Sir Bors at his left. Gerard thought he could close his eyes and recount every single thread in the tapestry, he had been staring at it for so long.

"I'm going to make a break for that cheese," Tyler muttered under his breath, two squires down. Mak, between them, snickered quietly. The cheese he referred to, a half-eaten yellow-washed wheel, was on the sideboard at the far end of the room, along with slices of meats, bread, and a scattering of dried fruits. The knights were able to get up and take food as they wished. None of the squires had that option, not while the council was in session. Nor without permission, which none of their masters had remembered to give, so caught up in the argument at hand.

Hunger aside, Gerard wasn't happy. And he didn't understand why. After the events of the past month—taking charge when the adults were all cast under a sleep-spell, and even facing down the king's sorceress half-sister—he had become the undisputed leader of the squires. There was even talk of him being knighted early. Not that it would happen right away. He had years to go yet. But the talk was enough to puff up his pride dangerously. Sir Lancelot, his hero, had even patted him on the shoulder approvingly when the story was told, and said that he himself could have done no better.

But greater than all that, Gerard had been invited by Arthur himself to join the knights on the Grail Quest when it finally rode out. For a fourteen-year-old squire, it was every dream coming true.

And yet . . .

"That, my king, is insane!"

And yet Gerard heartily wished he could be anywhere else right now. Even if it meant giving up his place on the Quest? No, probably not. But if suffering made a soul worthy to touch the Grail—the way some of the knights described—he was absolutely being readied for it.

"You dare?" Gerard was startled out of his morose thoughts when Sir Josia pounded on the table with one meaty fist, trying to drown out the knight across the table from him—both standing and gesturing excitedly.

"I dare because it is true! To leave Camelot now, when that sorceress has made such a blatant move against the king, is madness that must not go unchallenged! Sire, reconsider this! Send knights off, yes, if you must, but no such grand procession as was planned! And do not send the best of us when they are needed here!"

Sir Sagremor, an older knight, with the scars of battle on his face and arms, crashed his olivewood goblet onto the table. "Now is when we need the Grail most of all, you idiot! And only the finest of knights have any chance of finding it and bringing it home!"

"We need no cup to prove our worth! Least of all some cup that may not even exist!" Sir Lamorak said in disgust.

"Blasphemy!" Sir Galahad, normally the mildest of voices, shouted in outrage. He shoved his chair back across the stone floor as he stood up.

"*Your* blasphemy, maybe," Lamorak said in response. "I am no Christian, to worship a man on a tree."

The table erupted again, many voices competing against each other—not to be heard, but to drown the others out.

Through it all, Arthur sat in his grand chair at the Round Table. He leaned his bearded chin on his palm and watched intently as his knights shouted and swore and waved their arms to make their points. The din was almost unbearable. Gerard couldn't help but wonder how the king was able to hear anything, much less his own thoughts.

"Sire, please." Sir Kay, the king's foster brother and Gerard's uncle, spoke not in a shout, but a steady, even voice that carried to where the squires waited. "We *must* take action! One way or another, things must be decided. The Quest can be delayed no longer, else we look like fools and cowards."

Sir Kay was wise, and the king depended on his advice, but even *he* couldn't stop the shouting. Gerard decided it was never going to end. They would still be standing here—Arthur would still be listening to every viewpoint and opinion—when Gerard's hair was as gray as his master's, and nothing will have been decided. He couldn't help but compare all this to the way he, Newt, and Ailis had worked together on their quest to break Morgain's spell. They'd had differences, but they'd managed to do what needed to be done, without all this back and forth and back and forth with nobody listening to anyone else.

After some honest reflection, Gerard admitted that wasn't *entirely* true. They had argued more often than not. But when things had to be done, they were done.

Was it because the three of them didn't know enough to see other options? Or was it because they didn't have the time to sit and argue about it? And why did Arthur not put an end to all of this arguing and make a decision already—he was the *king*!

A slight movement from his master caught his eye. Gerard stepped forward to kneel by Sir Rheynold's chair, close enough to hear the murmured instructions.

"I was supposed to meet with the guardsmaster to discuss the Abmont estate levies, but there is no way that I will make that meeting as matters here stand. Tender him my regrets and ask him for a time of his convenience to reschedule."

In the past, Gerard might have been dismayed at the thought of having to miss any of the knights' discussions on a matter of such importance. Now he took the errand thankfully, aware of the envy of his fellow squires, still relegated to their posts on the off chance that their masters might need them as well.

"Take your time coming back, lad," one of the guards in the hallway said when Gerard pushed open the smaller door to leave. "Sounds as though they'll be at it for hours yet. Someone else can fetch your master his wine."

"Truth in that, and they'll need more wine, the way they're talking," another guard said with a laugh.

Gerard forced a smile at the comment, then turned and walked away. There was no great rush, true, but he would not malinger. That was the act of a raw page or a servant, not a squire. He would deliver Sir Rheynold's message to the master of the guards and return, although he might find time to stop by the kitchen and sneak something to eat before he did so. He was dedicated, not foolish.

And maybe someone in the kitchen would be able to carry a message for him to Ailis and Newt, to see if there was some way the three of them could arrange to see each other. He thought of Ailis especially. They had known each other all the years they had lived in Camelot, since they were children, and it seemed strange to be separated now, after seven days spent entirely in her company.

*   *   *

In the hallway, Ailis watched with wide eyes as a woman crouched over a globe of some sort, the size of a large porridge kettle. The globe was the source of the green glow that enveloped Morgain. Yes, it was Morgain. There was no mistaking that elegant form, even from the back. Inside the mystical globe there were figures, moving about. Ailis squinted, narrowing her eyes in an attempt to make out more detail.

Men, standing and sitting around . . . a great round table. Arthur's council table! She tried to stifle her startled gasp, but the sorceress was aware that she was being watched. Morgain immediately turned,

21

her long black hair swinging, her lovely, fine-boned face cast in a mask of anger that shifted quickly to surprise and then to a cunning sort of calculation.

Ailis knew that she should run, find help, alert the castle that Morgain was within the walls and was spying on the king. But something in the sorceress's eyes held her in place, even as she tried to resist.

"Witch-child."

"I am not!" Ailis tried to protest, but the words wouldn't come out of her mouth. She felt like a fish on a hook, being pulled helplessly to the fisher, and doom.

"Were you spying on me, witch-child? Sneaking and spying, drawn hither by . . . what?"

"I was running an errand," Ailis said, her jaw working again in response to Morgain's question. The sorceress was magicking her! Ailis tried to halt her own words, horrified at what she might say, but was unable to stop herself. "For one of the ladies of my queen's solar."

"You've access to the queen's company, then? Interesting. How very . . . interesting."

No! She would not say anything that might betray the queen, nothing that would endanger Camelot. She. Would. *Not.*

22

Something caused Morgain to lift her head just then, like a stag reacting to a distant hunter's horn, and the spell her eyes had on Ailis was broken. The girl turned to run, catching up her skirts in both hands, but an invisible hand caught at her shoulder, and pulled her backward.

"No, witch-child, I think you should come with me. I might have use of you."

"Nnnnnnnggghhhhh." Ailis tried to fight, but a low angry cry was all she could manage. Her heels dragged across the stone floor as she was pulled into the green glow. It seemed to be expanding, filling the hallway like a shadow, tinting the stone walls and darkening the floor like spilled blood. At the very last moment before the green energy overwhelmed her, Ailis felt the air being sucked from her lungs, and in that instant she was finally able to scream for help, for anyone to come. . . .

*   *   *

Gerard's steady walk slowed, almost without him noticing the change, and his hand went to his waist where his sword was not sheathed. No one carried a weapon inside Camelot's walls unless they were on guard duty. But something felt wrong, something that made him wish for solid steel. The sense of dissatisfaction and distaste from the council session had evaporated, replaced by unease and suspicion.

"You're getting as bad as Ailis, with her 'feelings,'" he told himself. "You're inside the most secure place on the entire island, surrounded by the finest warriors." *None of which were able to prevent a spell from being cast before.* His own thoughts worried at him.

There was nothing behind him, save a page dashing on in another direction much farther down the hallway, where it opened into an antechamber, and a serving girl was gossiping with two guards. Light from the wall lamps glinted off the pitcher she carried at her hip and the metal of the guards' byrnies that covered them from shoulder to waist. He thought briefly about calling to alert the guards, but what would he say to them? "I felt a chill, an unease?" They would mock him, and rightfully so, when it turned out to be a door left open ahead, or something equally foolish. "And this from the squire the king so praised?" he could imagine them joking in their sleeping quarters.

No. He would say nothing. There was nothing to say.

Clenching his jaw and pushing his shoulders back into a square set, the way he'd seen Arthur do, he walked forward into the intersection where the hallway he was in met up with several others. A page was curled up on a windowsill, using the daylight to study a scroll of some sort. Two maids worked to take down a tapestry that hung on the opposite wall while a different tapestry waited, rolled on the floor, to replace it.

Gerard walked past them all, nodding to the page when the boy looked up from his reading to see who it was. He didn't know all the pages, but this one seemed to know him.

"Good morn, Ger!"

The voice was familiar, yes, but the boy's name escaped him totally, so Gerard merely raised a hand in greeting, and walked on. He was almost at his destination; through this antechamber, past the stairs which led to the cellars, and two doors down, was the walkway to the guardroom, where the master of the guard would be found for receipt of Sir Rheynold's message. Same time spent getting back, even if he did pause at the kitchen, and he would probably find the same argument he had left still going on.

"Months of boredom, followed by a mad dash across the marshes in the midst of the night," Gerard said out loud, quoting what his master had said years ago when describing the life of a knight. As a page he hadn't believed it, thinking that every moment of a knight's life must be excitement and derring-do.

But it was so. The majority of life was a slow, dreary slog through the things that must be done. Gerard supposed that was true even if you were the king. And that included listening to everyone argue about something, even if you've already made up your mind about what you're going to do.

He shivered again, a sudden ice-cold finger sliding down his spine in a deeply unpleasant way. Without thinking, he turned away from the hallway that led to his destination, and instead went left, finding himself running down one of the routes that servants used when they needed to move fast and stay out of sight.

Ailis had taught him about those ways, the semi-secret passages throughout Camelot that none of the nobles knew about. It had been a game when they were children, to race across the castle without using any of the main corridors or hallways. It had been years since he'd done that, true, but he didn't remember any of the passages having such a green cast to the stone, no matter what time of day or night.

Something is wrong. Something is very wrong, was all he had time to think before he turned a corner and was almost blinded by the intense green glow filling the passage.

Danger! His senses screamed at him, every muscle instinctively readying itself for combat, the way he had been trained to react. The glow burned, made him flinch away. *Magic! Danger!*

In the instant before his eyes shut in self-defense, his brain caught the image of Ailis, her hands reaching for him, her face terrified, as she was sucked backward into the heart of the glow.

Behind Ailis, her face the same diamond perfection he remembered from their last encounter—the sorceress Morgain!

"Ailis!" he shouted, fighting to move forward into the glow, reaching out for her, trying to find her. He had to save her! But even as he ran forward, something Newt had said during their adventure came back to him: *"Charging in blind is not the act of a hero, not if you don't know what's going on."*

It was just enough to make him hesitate, and then the glow was gone. The passageway was empty. No glow. No Morgain. No Ailis.

Gerard stared for a moment in disbelief. *How?* How did Morgain get in here? And what was Ailis doing with her?

Gerard scanned the space again, as though hoping that Ailis would reappear out of thin air or that his eyes had been playing tricks on him.

But the hallway remained empty. With a curse, Gerard turned on his heels and ran for the Council Room.

Newt was right. As much as he'd wanted to follow Ailis into that glow, it would have been the act of a fool. Morgain was dangerous. This was a matter for older, wiser, more experienced men. Ailis's life—and the security of Camelot—depended on it!

* * *

Falling and rising at the same time, buffeted by terrible winds, spinning and expanding into an infinite space. No sense of place or time, no sense of anything except turning and spinning and the endless falling and the endless rising, all at once, until she thought she might throw up. Aware of the bile in her throat, she struck out, her fingers dragging on nothingness that was somehow solid, a thick rope of something that shimmered under her grasp and then disappeared. Other ropes appeared under her fingers, and she grabbed and let them go, categorizing each one even as they were pulled away or faded from her grasp, until a pattern began to emerge.

One line went thus, and another went there, and when they moved in such a way the winds came from below, and when they moved like that, the winds came from the side, as though they were being rushed by pulleys through enormous external doors.

She could almost sense how they worked, how they opened and closed. The pattern shimmered in her mind, diagrams appearing on a slate; dry scratchings that began to shimmer with color and light the longer she worked at them. Reaching out to learn more, to touch more, her hand was struck down by something . . . someone? A quick harsh blow stung, and she cried out, sound in the wind-locked emptiness. Then a cool mint fog settled over her awareness, wiping the slate clean. . . .

THREE

Gerard paid no attention to dignity or manners on his way back to the Council Room. It mattered more that he got there as quickly as possible, not how many people saw him racing down hallways and across courtyards like an untamed page.

Morgain. *Morgain in the castle!* Was the sorceress here to make another attempt at preventing the Quest from riding out? Or was she finally making an actual strike against King Arthur?

And what did she want with Ailis? Was it revenge for Ailis's part in breaking her sleep-spell? Or something more—something worse?

Despite the training squires were given on a daily basis, Gerard was winded when he got back to the Council Room. Riding and fighting, even in armor, did not prepare you for sprinting through hallways in such urgent circumstances.

"Hold up, lad. Can't go back in there gasping like a landed fish," one of the guards said, placing a fatherly hand on his shoulder. "What's the cause of you rushing back, against all advice? Nothing's going on in there at all, save squabbling and gossip, since the king's been called away."

That got Gerard's attention. "What? He has?" Had someone already carried news of Morgain's appearance and her thefting of Ailis out from under their noses?

"A rider came in from the northern Marches. One of Arthur's snoops thinks the lord there is planning to use our recent difficulties"—the adults had taken to speaking of the spell as a "recent difficulty"—"to break away and be his own master, rather than pay fealty come the spring."

The one thing Gerard had learned, to his astonishment, was that the common guardsmen often knew details—not gossip, but facts—sooner and more accurately than even the wisest knight. So he did not question what they told him. His shoulders slumped. He had a better chance of winning this year's tournament melee single-handed than he did of reaching Arthur now. Dissent along the Marches was what the

Quest was to prevent in the first place; the Quest would show the lords in the lands beyond where Arthur held sole rule, who owed their allegiances to King Arthur, that he was indeed the man to rule them. And this incipient rebellion was exactly what Morgain would be hoping to provoke by her actions.

So now Gerard—and everyone else—knew what was going to happen. Arthur would not only go forward with the Quest, but he would do it in as grand and public a manner as possible. He had no choice.

But Gerard wondered, wouldn't he need to keep men close at home, too, in case the Marcher Lords did try to rebel?

He shook the thought off. It wasn't his concern. His immediate goal was to find someone who could get the king's ear and tell him that Morgain had been inside the castle walls and taken Ailis!

"Many thanks," he said to the guards, and ducked inside the Council Room. He had failed to deliver his master's message, and that would earn him a cuff against the head. But Sir Rheynold would be able to help him, once he knew the urgency.

Sure enough, the scene inside was no less noisy than before, only now the knights were arguing directly with each other, rather than trying to make a show for the king.

"Sir?" Gerard came up beside Sir Rheynold, who was talking with several knights of his generation, older men who had originally served King Arthur's father, Uther Pendragon.

"Yes, Gerard, what is—" The knight took in Gerard's expression and his sweat-beaded face. He took his squire by the shoulder and walked him a few steps away.

"What is it?"

Gerard told him.

*   *   *

Ten minutes later, Sir Rheynold and Gerard were standing outside the offices of the seneschal, the man who ran Camelot's household business for King Arthur.

"Have you a message for Master Godrain?" The young clerk who served the seneschal was barely old enough to have grown his first downy yellow beard. He looked as though a chick had gone to sleep on his chin, but he glanced at Sir Rheynold as though the older man was a servant. He didn't even acknowledge Gerard.

"I would speak with him directly," Sir Rheynold said, refusing to be put off. He stood in front of the clerk's desk, his arms folded over his broad chest, and stared back, his leathery, heavily lined features unyielding.

"I am afraid that will not—"

"It will," Sir Rheynold said, in an equally calm tone. "And it will be, *now*." When the clerk would have protested further, the knight merely glanced at Gerard, as though to say, "This is how you handle such annoyances." Rheynold walked around the desk, his stride vigorous enough to take him to the inner chamber's door before the clerk could leap to his feet and try and stop him.

One hard knock on the door, and Sir Rheynold was casting it open. He walked inside as though it were the entrance to his own bedchamber.

"Godrain!"

The seneschal looked up from his ledgers, then stood, rising and rising and rising from his seat until he towered over the knight. Gerard, standing in the doorway behind his master, thought that Master Godrain would have made a splendid giant, had there been any flesh on those long bones. Instead of being impressive, however, he merely looked hungry.

"I will assume you have good reason to come barging in here like this," the man said, his dry voice matching his dry complexion.

"My squire saw Morgain in the castle." Rheynold reached back and caught Gerard by the shoulder without looking, and dragged him forward.

"What?" Godrain blinked several times in confusion, as though that would make the words suddenly make sense. Then he looked closely at Gerard. "You're the boy who broke the spell."

"I was one of them, yes," Gerard said.

"And you think you saw the sorceress Morgain here? In Camelot?"

"Yes." Though he didn't just *think* he saw her, he wanted to add. He *knew* what Morgain looked like, better than anyone in this room, probably better than anyone in the entire kingdom, save Arthur and Merlin.

"She was here. Spying, maybe. Or working some worse mischief. I saw her, and there was this green light, a spell, probably. And she took Ailis!"

"Are you sure your boy here knows what he's saying?" Godrain asked Rheynold, as though Gerard hadn't spoken.

"I trust Gerard implicitly," the knight said. In

any other situation, Gerard would have nearly burst with pride to hear his master say that. But now, the teenager could barely restrain himself from grabbing the seneschal by his robes and shaking him like a terrier would a rat. Every moment they delayed, who knew what was happening to Ailis!

"Still. How can we be certain? The idea that Merlin's protections are not enough to keep her out seems . . . unlikely." Godrain's smile and tone suggested what he thought of Merlin despite his words. "A half-hysterical boy, no matter how well he performed during the recent difficulties . . ."

"The king himself praised Gerard's cool head and thinking," Rheynold said, as though he himself had never called Gerard flighty, or foolish, or hotheaded over the years.

"Please!" Gerard broke into the conversation, not caring that he was being rude. "She has Ailis!"

"Gerard! I know that you are upset, but it's not as though we can do anything for the girl right now," said Sir Rheynold.

"Nor is there any reason to do so," the seneschal said thoughtfully, folding himself back into his chair and looking hard at the two of them. "You say that Morgain was aware of your discovery of her?"

"I . . . I think so."

"But you can't be sure? This is important, boy, so be as certain as you can."

He tried to think back, trying not to focus on Ailis's face, but the expression of the woman standing behind her. Other than the sorceress's beauty, which was unforgettable, what had she looked like? "I . . . don't think so. No. She seemed . . . satisfied. Not worried or startled."

"Good. If she does not know you saw her, then she will be complacent, perhaps smug. She will be careless, and that may give us an advantage."

"But Ailis!" Gerard couldn't believe what he was hearing. Was this how Camelot protected the innocent? Defended their people? What about Arthur's code of chivalry?

"One girl is of no great importance," Godrain said coldly. "Finding a way to put that witch on the defensive; *that* is important. The king was willing to give Morgain benefit of the doubt before, but the spell has damaged his desire to protect her. This may be the final blow."

"But—"

"Gerard! Sit down."

For the first time in his life, in the years he had

spent as part of Sir Rheynold's household, Gerard locked gazes with his master and refused a direct order.

"I won't let you abandon Ailis." It was a knife into his heart to defy Sir Rheynold. But if he was not true to his companions now, how could he ever hope to be a good and just knight? How could he even think of taking his place on the Quest for the Grail if he were not true to his heart?

"Boy, we will not tell you again—" Master Godrain began, only to be interrupted by a commotion from the doorway. The clerk's voice was raised, protesting against a deeper voice. The words were muffled, but the flurry of noise and excitement stirred Gerard's hopes.

The clerk was trying to bar the doorway. Then he stopped and, with a resigned sigh, stepped aside. Merlin brushed past him, intentionally pushing the young man away, and walked in.

"I don't have time for that," he said over his shoulder to the annoyed clerk. "And I don't have time to turn you into a rat. Rats are beginning to bore me. Rabbits. Rabbits are good. And if one or three end up in the stewpot, it's not as though they were doing any good interfering with decent people's lives anyway. Might as well feed some folk by example, as it were."

His gaze fell upon Gerard, and the perpetual scowl underneath that hawk's beak of a nose seemed to lighten a touch. "Just the youngster I think I was coming to see. Or have I seen you already? No, that was before, this is now. My brains are still a bit scrambled. Too cold for me, too cold," and he gave a dramatic shudder under the heavy gray wool cape that had been flung across his shoulders.

Merlin seemed to have a fondness for Ailis, speaking to her directly, his voice in her head even over great distances. To have him back now, when Ailis needed someone to champion her, it seemed so much a miracle Gerard could only promise himself that he would say his prayers more regularly from now on.

Merlin's attention turned back to Gerard. "Now, I think we have matters to discuss, yes? Something you needed to tell me? Or was it that I had something to tell you?" His heavy eyebrows drew together in a scowl that Sir Rheynold seemed to find threatening, though Gerard felt almost reassured. Merlin was reputed to live backward in time, which left him sounding perpetually mad, but after a while it was a madness that almost made sense. Merlin knew that Gerard needed to see him, that it was important, and that he had the answer Gerard needed. More important: Merlin was here, and the king's enchanter outranked a seneschal.

"You may not interfere here, old man," Godrain said, not even bothering to rise from his chair again, as though insulting him could make Merlin go away. "In the matter of . . . such matters, I make the decisions as to whom the king will see."

"Indeed you do," Merlin said. "Far be it from me to interfere in such weighty matters as those. In fact, this boy should not be here at all, filling your valuable time with his news. I shall take him away at once, immediately, if not sooner. Boy, with me!"

Afterward, Gerard could never quite remember how they got from Godrain's chambers to Merlin's quarters. There was a blurred memory of Sir Rheynold, left standing in the chaos, and a swirl of servants welcoming Merlin back as they went about their business, but it seemed a matter of seconds to move from one end of the castle to another. Was it magic? Or just the confusion that always seemed to surround the enchanter wherever he went?

However the means, Gerard soon found himself

in a corridor that was dry and dusty and clearly off-limits to most of the castle's population: Merlin's private chambers. Merlin opened the door with a low muttered incantation, ushered Gerard in, and deposited him in a surprisingly comfortable wooden chair set against one wall. The squire leaned back into it, feeling the wood warm under his backside. He had almost caught his breath when the lions' heads at the end of the wooden armrests turned and snarled at him. Gerard jumped, but when they didn't do more than snarl, he relaxed again. Magic. He was beginning to understand Newt's objections to it.

The enchanter was busy dropping a number of dubious-looking leather sacks into a wooden chest and locking it securely. That done, he turned and looked at the squire. Merlin's face was lined with exhaustion and his eyes were even more hooded than usual, but there was nothing slack in his attitude. Despite everything, Gerard still felt reassured. This time, Merlin was here. This time, the enchanter could make everything right.

"Now, what happened?"

"I was running an errand for Sir Rheynold, and there was . . . something felt wrong." He hadn't told that to the seneschal, but he had to give Merlin the whole story. Merlin wouldn't laugh at him. Well, he might, but he would also know if the feeling of unease was important or not. And if it was important, then Merlin needed to know.

"Wrong like a stomachache wrong, or a toothache?"

Gerard blinked in surprise at the question, then replied, "A toothache."

"And then you saw Morgain?"

"Then I saw a glow. Not right away, after I'd gone a little farther down the hall. But—"

Merlin held up a hand abruptly, his eyes narrowing. The squire halted, confused. "Stop gawking outside and come in, fool child," the enchanter said in a deeply cranky tone.

The wooden door to the hallway swung open and a familiar head of disordered black hair looked inside.

"You *are* back!" Newt said in satisfaction. "How did you escape from Nimue? Did they tell you what Arthur said when we told him? And . . . Gerard? They never told me you were with him—what's wrong?"

"In, fool of a horse-boy, in!" Merlin said, and something invisible yanked Newt into the room, and shut the door firmly behind him.

FOUR

"How did you know to come here?" Gerard asked his friend. He watched Newt move a pile of strange metal blocks off a bench and place them carefully on the floor before he sat down. They looked harmless enough, but in an enchanter's work-room, you assumed nothing.

Newt's shaggy black hair had already grown out of the trim someone had forced on him when they were formally presented to the king after their adventure. The brown pants and lighter-colored shirt he wore bore definite signs of his equine charges. In other words, he looked like Newt—solid, dependable, and practical to the end.

"I told him, of course," Merlin said, as though giving up on expecting common sense out of either boy. The enchanter stalked over to his desk and began digging through the untidy piles of parchments and scripts there in search of something.

Newt nodded his head in agreement. "I was exercising one of the horses, that new bay they brought in—and a right overeager beast it is, Gerard. Don't let them put any ham-handed novice up on him or they'll both be sorry. Anyway, I heard Merlin in my head. Is that how you spoke to Ailis? No wonder she was unnerved! And Merlin told me to get myself over here in a hurry. So I did."

He might look like the familiar old Newt, but he didn't sound like him. Gerard had never heard the stable boy quite so agitated, even during the worst moments of their mad ride to break the sleep-spell, the month before.

Perhaps Newt's nervousness was because Merlin had used magic on him. The stable boy, while not denying magic's usefulness, had always been uncomfortable around it. Gerard had wondered about that, especially when Ailis started to show signs of mastering it.

"Merlin, what about Ailis? You have to get her back!"

"What?" Newt stopped babbling and stared first at Gerard, then Merlin, then back at Gerard. "Ailis?

Who took Ailis? When? How? Why isn't anyone doing anything about it?"

"Morgain, just now, we don't know yet, and we are," Merlin answered. He snapped his fingers and paused from his search of the desk. A chair slid along the floor behind him, stopping just shy of hitting the enchanter in the back of the knees, and Merlin sat down with the perfect confidence of someone who knew that the chair would indeed be in position for him. "Gerard. Continue your story."

The squire took a deep breath, settling his mind as best he could, focusing on nothing but the exact events in question. Newt ran one hand through his hair, raking it back impatiently, and let his gaze settle on Gerard's face as though afraid he might miss even one syllable of the story.

"I told you, I saw a glow in the hallway. In the servants' ways, not the main hall."

Merlin nodded. Of course someone like him would know of all hidden ways in the castle.

"The light . . . it was green, like . . . well, not like anything I can tell you." He had no idea how to describe that color or the sensations that the glow sent through him. But Merlin was expecting it. Ailis was relying on him. "And . . . there was this sense of terrible wrongness. So I went forward and I saw her."

"Morgain?" Merlin asked, leaning forward.

"No, Ailis. She was facing me, and scared, and the glow was all around her like . . . like a bug caught in tree sap. It was only after that I saw Morgain standing behind her."

"And then?" Merlin prompted.

"And then it got so bright I had to close my eyes. It hurt. And when I opened them again, they were . . . gone." Gerard felt horrible having to admit it, even worse than he'd felt at the time. Then, he'd been so startled and so angry. Now, with time to think . . . he was scared. He kept wondering what he could have done, what he should have done. What a knight—better trained, wiser, smarter, braver— might have done. He was supposed to protect the innocent, not stand by while they were taken out from under his very nose. He had failed. He had hesitated like a page waiting for instructions.

That memory made his indignation at the seneschal's attitude rise again. "Godrain wants us to do nothing, to let Morgain think she's not been detected."

"No doubt Godrain is an officious fool, but in this case his thinking is sound." Merlin tapped his chin thoughtfully while he spoke. "Morgain overconfident would be an easier target than Morgain feeling hunted. She has already been taken down once in recent weeks; her pride must have driven her to make another foray."

"You're saying we should just leave Ailis with her? In the hands of that . . . woman?" Gerard was outraged. Who knew what was happening to her as they sat here and argued.

"I am saying no such thing. Sit down, both of you."

Gerard hadn't even noticed that both he and Newt had gotten to their feet.

"But—"

"Sit."

They sat.

"I know you're worried. So am I. Ailis struck hard at Morgain, last they met, and the sorceress is not the sort to forgive that. I said that Morgain overconfident is a good thing for us. And it is. Because once again, boys, there's hard truth coming. I gave Nimue's little icehouse the slip because I knew I was needed here."

Gerard frowned, wondering if it was so simple to escape, why hadn't Merlin left his icy prison before, when the three of them needed him?

Merlin continued, "And now, the gods above and

below, with Marcher Lords causing trouble and threatening Arthur's hold on the title of High King—the only thing that keeps those damned Romans out of our lands—and Morgain is stirring in her jealousy again. Why that woman cannot be content with the lot she was given in life I'll never know. There's no way I can leave here to search for Ailis, not even for a day. Arthur needs me by his side to give counsel, or to be seen giving counsel, or to warn off those who might otherwise interfere. That is my sworn vow, and I cannot break it."

"But—" Newt began. Once again, Merlin wasn't going to be able to help them. What good was an enchanter if he couldn't fix things with a snap of his fingers or a wave of that birchwood wand he sometimes carried?

"But the thought of young Ailis in Morgain's clutches is a matter of some concern, yes. I sent her from the safety of Camelot's walls once before—with great reluctance, yes—because I knew that I would always be able to reach you three through her."

"So it *was* you speaking to her!" Newt said in a burst of satisfaction.

"Of course it was, fool. Who else could it have been?"

Newt looked as though he wanted to respond, but stopped himself. Now was not the time to mention their—or Ailis's—doubts about the voice.

"I don't want to take on any new students—I can't, until Nimue gets over whatever fit of pique she's in—and I certainly don't want to take on a girl-child right now. But Ailis has the ability, and I hate to see waste, so I gave her a push or two in the right direction when I could. None of that's important now, boys, except that Morgain is no fool, and she will have seen what I saw." He paused, took a breath, and calmed himself down. "And, knowing Morgain, she will find some way to use it to her own benefit."

"So Ailis *is* in danger," Gerard said. "But you have to stay here. To advise Arthur and keep him safe, in case he has to ride out to face the marcher lords." Newt gave him a look, like he was stating the obvious, but Gerard wanted to make sure that there were no twitchy, slippery miscommunications here.

"And to keep Camelot safe while he is away, whatever my king decides." Merlin nodded in response to Gerard's words, his face suddenly bearing the weight of his countless decades. "Yes. In either case, I am not free right now to go after Morgain, drat her for bad timing. But if she is overconfident, not expecting immediate retaliation, then we have a chance for something sneaky, something with a chance of actually working."

"She's a sorceress," Newt said in protest.

"Yes, she is. But the only people in the castle other than myself who have any real, practical, useful knowledge of Morgain's magic and how to combat it are—"

"Us," Gerard said, a heavy feeling settling into his chest. A practical knowledge of magic, maybe. But knowing how to combat it? He wasn't so sure. Morgain was unlikely to allow them to simply leave, unharmed, the way she did the first time. Then she had been willing to let an opening gambit fail. Cross someone twice, Gerard knew, and they were even less likely to forgive.

"Us?" Newt repeated, his voice cracking the way Gerard's used to when he was particularly upset or angry.

The enchanter nodded, grave-faced. "Yes, you."

So much for Gerard's dreams of traveling with the knights on their great Quest. Ailis was more important, of course, but it still hurt to know that— the king's promise or no—if the Quest set off before they returned with Ailis it would leave without him.

Decisions, boy, he could hear Sir Rheynold saying. *Every turn in life is a decision.*

Newt swallowed hard, then nodded. "Right. Defeating a sorceress in her den. Done it once already, why not twice? Hey, maybe we can make it a yearly event, like one of your tourneys." The joke didn't even come close to being funny.

"We need to discuss this with Arthur, but quickly," Merlin said, catching both their gazes to make sure they were listening. "And quietly, quietly. The fact that Morgain was able to gain access to the castle makes me think she may have helpers I did not know about, even inside my own walls, and that is not a comforting thought." Merlin could play the fool when he chose to, but in this instance he was deadly serious. "Come, both of you. Time to talk, and then time to move."

Newt stood up. But Gerard hesitated, the fingers of his left hand absently stroking the mane of one of the carved lions, feeling the odd rumble of a wooden purr resonating throughout the chair.

"Gerard?"

He looked up, directly into Merlin's face looming over him. Those eyes were deep-set with exhaustion, but that hawk's glare was tempered, somehow, with understanding.

"You did the right thing." Merlin wasn't very good at giving compliments, and it showed. "You didn't do anything foolish. Rest easy on that score; none here could have done better, and many would have done worse."

"But I couldn't save her."

"You couldn't stop her from being taken, no. The first step in wisdom, lad, is knowing when you're in trouble, and not doing something bullheaded and getting yourself killed in answer. I'd rather have a dozen of you than a full army of foolhardy heroes."

Gerard wasn't sure if that was a compliment or not. He chose to believe that Merlin meant it as one.

They went out the door, Merlin in the lead, then Gerard, and then Newt. The stable boy had arrived ready to go wherever it was they would have to go, do whatever they had to do, as Merlin asked him. Even before he knew that Ailis's life was at stake; even if it led them to more magic.

But not without planning, preparation, and all the support Camelot could give them.

"Hang on, Ailis," Newt whispered. "Hang on, don't antagonize Morgain. We're coming."

* * *

Ailis woke to a vague sense of dizziness, as though she had slipped, but not fallen; been dropped from a terrible height, and never landed. And yet she was comfortable, for all the disorientation she felt.

"Mama?"

Even as the words were out of her mouth, Ailis knew the sense of comfort around her was a false one. Her mother had been dead for eight years now, mother and father both, and nobody in Camelot, dear though they might be, had ever become a second mother to her.

Something's not right, she thought. *Why do I feel so strange? Why can't I think properly?*

Opening her eyes slowly, Ailis was struck by how clean the ceiling was. Normally ceilings were darker, as years of use had coated the pale gray stones of Camelot with an overlay of soot. But this ceiling had been freshly washed for some reason. The stone gleamed almost white, even in the dim candlelight, and the gilding around the corners of the bed—

Ailis sat up suddenly, ignoring the rush of dizziness and the sudden sharp pain in her left temple. *Bed? Gilding? Ow!*

"Good. You are awake. Mistress will be pleased."

A hazy shape glided forward and handed Ailis a

silver cup filled with some liquid. She took it and drank it down without question, still too confused and puzzled to question, distracted by the pain in her head and the strangeness of her surroundings.

It was water, clear and fresh and cool—the most refreshing thing Ailis could remember ever tasting. The cup was hammered silver, almost warm to the touch, with some sort of design traced into the metal around the lip.

"Ah, good," the figure said, taking the cup away from her before she could look at it more closely. The servant seemed almost smoky around the edges, although that might have been Ailis's inability to focus.

Something . . . strange is happening.

"Rest now. Mistress will be in to see you soon. Rest."

Mistress? Ailis knew that there were things that she should be asking, things that she should be doing. But her thirst satisfied, the thick down-filled bed called to her, enticed her, and she sank back into it without protest. Her eyes closed and her body slid back down into sleep.

Nothing that felt this comfortable could be bad, could it?

FIVE

"So what *did* Arthur say when you told him where I was?" Merlin asked Newt as they walked through the castle. They were heading for the main audience chamber where Merlin claimed Arthur would be.

Newt shrugged off Merlin's question. He certainly wasn't going to tell Merlin the truth, which was that the king had sighed and said, "Some day, that woman is going to get him into real trouble."

"Insolent brat," Merlin muttered at the boy's silence, and Newt felt a grin start to form despite the tension of the moment. Ailis had said that Merlin was like a kettle; so long as it was letting off steam, everything was all right. It was when the kettle ran dry and silent that you had trouble.

Soon Merlin was pushing his way through the

crowds of people waiting to see the king. When they were in the king's presence, Gerard and Newt kneeled, and Merlin whispered something to the king. Next they were following Arthur out of the chamber and into his private study. It was all a blur. Newt tried not to stumble over his own feet or let anyone realize that a mere stable boy, still stinking of straw and sweat, was moving among them.

The king closed the door behind them, stopping at least one courtier from following them in. His heavy robes of state flowed around him as he moved. "All right, my Merlin. Tell me what I need to know that is so important that you drag me away from matters of war."

Merlin was clearly used to doing just that. He held up his hand and began ticking points off, finger by finger.

"Morgain was spotted inside the castle. Morgain was doing some sort of magic within the castle. Morgain disappeared from the castle when she was discovered, and took with her a member of your household, the girl-child Ailis."

"Ailis?" Arthur looked puzzled for a moment. Then his heavy-set brows relaxed as he placed the name. "The servant-girl who found the talismans with . . . these two youngsters. They're the ones who saw Morgain?"

Merlin nodded.

Newt shifted uneasily, wondering if the king was going to blame them for bringing bad news. Or, worse, think they had made it up, eager for more attention the way younglings sometimes did. He hadn't seen anything at all, but if Gerard said he had, then he had. And with Ailis missing . . . something was very wrong. "King Arthur *has* to believe—"

"He does," Arthur said. Newt flushed a deep red, having just realized he had said that last thought out loud. "But there is a difference between believing, and acting on that belief.

"Why must my sister pester me so!" Arthur added in frustration. He began to pace back and forth in the small room. "Any other king would have had her killed the first time she stood against him. Does she think I am weak to push me so? I gave her everything I could, preserved her when others"—he glared at Merlin—"would have had her exiled, or worse. What drives her to such insanity?"

The king looked older than he had that morning listening to the Knights of the Round Table arguing, Gerard thought. That had been the face of the king among his loyal men. This was the face of the High King, the overlord of Britain, with all the pain and responsibility that came with the title.

"Sire," Merlin began, but Arthur waved him off.

"I know, old fox, I know. We need to discover what she's up to, and this is the perfect opportunity. But I need you here."

"And I need to be here, sire." Merlin's voice was oddly humble, the way it only was when speaking to his king. "But these boys do not. And, perhaps, a guide to go with them, an older knight, to even the balance of their youth. Who can we send . . ."

"Caedor?" Arthur suggested, clearly running through the list of knights in his mind.

"Hmmm. Yes. Caedor. He's a loyal dog, he is. That might be enough to turn the tide and ensure that whatever Morgain is planning, we are ready for it."

Arthur turned and looked at the two teenagers, his brow furrowing as he considered them. "They did well enough when we needed them, yes," he said slowly. "But the conditions were vastly different then. To send them up against Morgain directly . . . even stout hearts are no match for her. I know this all too well, and to my own loss." It was as though Arthur had forgotten the two boys were in the room at all.

"Stout hearts alone, no," Merlin agreed. "But their strength—and my cunning. And your wisdom."

"You can give them that?" Arthur looked intrigued, but not surprised.

"I can, sire. Some small measure to draw upon, at least."

"And it will not lessen your cunning?"

"Nor your wisdom," the enchanter said.

Arthur shook his head. "Of that I have little faith these days. But if it will not harm, and may possibly help, then do it, wizard mine. Do it quickly. I have little time to spare, and they have none at all."

Merlin nodded, then turned to beckon the boys closer. "Stand thus." He arranged them shoulder to shoulder between himself and the king. He looked to Arthur for permission, which was granted with a small nod. Merlin opened his hand, palm to the ceiling, and a short, sharp knife appeared. The handle was white bone, carved with strange figures and runes. Gerard and Newt thought of the tracings on the map they had used to track down the talismans during their last adventure. Merlin's handwriting. That was reassuring.

"Relax, boys. I haven't lost anyone yet doing this," Merlin said, seeing the tension on their faces.

"And how many times have you done it?" Newt asked, cheeky even as he went pale at the realization that he was about to be magicked.

"Oh, once, maybe," Merlin said. He raised the blade so that the candlelight filling the room was reflected in the metal, blinding them for an instant. Then the blade came down against Newt's left cheekbone, scoring him lightly. Before he could yelp at the pain, the knife was raised up again, and brought down on Gerard's right. The squire stood silent. *Blood-magic.*

Then Merlin turned the blade on Arthur's offered hands, grazing the king's palms so carefully that only a small trace of blood seeped from each hair-thin wound. Arthur, from his position behind them, reached around and cupped each boy's face so that his wounds matched to theirs, the faintest trickle of blood mingling.

As he did so, Merlin covered Arthur's hands with his own and muttered something in a low, raspy voice that wasn't quite his, in a language that was liquid-sounding and almost familiar. Newt tensed momentarily, then relaxed. There came a time when you had to trust someone.

"And thus it was done," Merlin said, releasing Arthur's hands and stepping back. The king was slower to let go, as though reluctant to remove his protection, however small it might be. Finally he did, and stepped around and faced the two boys.

"You do this from the finest of motives," he said to them. "Love of a friend. Concern for a kingdom. Belief in your cause. To that I can only add the pride of a king and wish you Godspeed and good luck."

And then, to the shock of both Gerard and Newt, he hugged them—a quick, almost brusque hug—and left the room.

"You've been in the presence of a great leader," Merlin said. "A great leader, who would be greater still were he a lesser man. And now you need to be on your way and better outfitted than before. We can do this properly this time. Horses, supplies, weapons . . . Come on then, what are you waiting for?"

Newt and Gerard looked at each other and, despite their concern for Ailis, they both grinned. On their first quest they had been completely isolated, the adults all asleep under Morgain's spell. Now, even if they were on their own, they would not be *alone*. Arthur and Merlin were both there for them. They both reached up to touch the cuts already forming tender scabs on their faces.

"What do you think he did to us?" Newt asked as

they followed in Merlin's wake, dodging the servants and courtiers he sent running with a barked command or wave of his hand. "It didn't feel like anything."

"I don't know. We'll find out soon enough, I'll wager," Gerard said in return. "You're taking it awfully calm, someone working magic on you."

"As my king commands," Newt said, irritated. "Knights aren't the only ones who understand that."

"I never said they were. I just—"

But Newt had already put on a burst of speed and caught up with Merlin, clearly not wanting to talk to Gerard anymore. The squire sighed. Whenever he tried to insult the stable boy, the words just rolled off his back. But when he didn't mean anything by it, *then* Newt took offense.

"Idiot stable boy," he muttered. Then he put on speed himself, catching up with the others as they started down the stairs that led to the kitchen. Once they had Ailis back home and safe he and Newt needed to have a few things out, starting with the fact that they were friends, however unlikely, and friends didn't assume the worst of each other. Right now, if it wasn't going to interfere with what they had to do—and he couldn't see how it would—then it just wasn't important enough to worry about.

SIX

"I think I preferred leaving without fanfare," Newt said, frustration evident in his voice.

"I cannot believe that we're traveling in such a haphazard, unbecoming fashion," Sir Caedor grumbled.

Gerard exchanged an ironic look with Newt. The stable boy had bet the squire half a crown that Sir Caedor would not be pleased with their arrangements.

"Why does he have to come with us?" Newt muttered, shifting on the back of Loyal, the horse he had taken on their previous journey. Less handsome than Gerard's gelding or Sir Caedor's mare, Belinda, Loyal was well-named, and Newt would take no other. Arthur had said that one who worked in the stables was expected to be the best judge of horseflesh and commended him on his choice.

"Because I say you must," Merlin replied, even though it hadn't really been a question. He appeared between the two horses and riders where he had not been an instant before, making all four of them start in surprise. Gerard quickly turned his horse's head aside when the animal tried to take a bite out of the enchanter's shoulder.

"I know, he grumbles," the enchanter continued. "But Sir Caedor is a good man, for all that his tourney-fighting days are past, and his experience will complement your natural gifts."

Gerard had to admit the truth of that. Sir Caedor might be of an age with Sir Rheynold, but he had not let his years turn him into a stay-at-home. There was strength left in Sir Caedor's arm and courage in his heart. So long as he did not assume that time and experience alone made him the leader of this rescue attempt, then they would have no trouble at all.

Gerard did not think for a moment, however, that Sir Caedor would accept taking orders from a squire. And from the expression on Newt's face, he doubted that his friend thought so, either. But Merlin commanded, with the weight of Arthur's voice in his, and so you accepted. Hopefully Sir Caedor knew that, as well.

The horses shifted, the pages having finished their last-minute checks. The mule carrying their extra supplies lifted first one leg then the other, indicating a desire to be off.

"Will we be beginning our journey, then?" Sir Caedor shouted, kneeing his mare forward to join the three of them. "Or is there some unknown-to-me reason we yet delay?"

Gerard sighed. Why had Merlin placed *him* in charge, and not Sir Caedor?

"There is indeed reason yet to wait," a rich alto voice said from above them. All four looked up, and Newt almost fell off his horse. Queen Guinevere stood on the balcony above the courtyard where they were gathered. Several of her ladies-in-waiting clustered around her like pastel wildflowers to her golden rose. "I have come to see our brave questers off if they would care to wait for me."

"My lady, we would," Sir Caedor said, bowing to her as gallantly as one could while on horseback. Gerard didn't mind him taking the lead here, not at all. He had no idea what you said to a queen. He wasn't even sure he knew how to bow properly.

He didn't have much time to think about it before Queen Guinevere was coming through the courtyard archway. She was tall and fair, with golden hair coiled about her head and a deep blue gown draped about her body in a way that made her seem even more regal. She was supposed to be the most beautiful woman in the entire kingdom. Gerard thought she was very pretty, but preferred Ailis's lively expressions and energy to the Queen's slow and studied movements.

"Jenny," Merlin said with unflattering familiarity. "You're late. As usual." She smiled at him, the indulgent smile someone has for a much-loved but often impossible brother.

"My queen," Sir Caedor said, sliding down from his horse to make another impressive bow. She gave him a more reserved smile than the one granted to Merlin, then turned to face Newt and Gerard, who followed Caedor's lead and slid down from their horses as well.

"You go to rescue my Allison."

"Yes, my queen," Gerard said. Newt managed a stout nod.

Guinevere's smile warmed again, and she gestured to the young girl who had followed her out. The girl, dark-haired and pale-skinned, held out a small box from which Guinevere removed two silver bands.

"A token for Allison's champions," she said, offering the first band to Gerard, the second to Newt. After a moment's hesitation, Newt took his and slid it up on his arm the same way Gerard had. Each band was worked with a delicate pattern of small blossoms winding its way around, and a dark green stone set in the clasp.

"Wear them with honor and courage. I know that you will bring my Allison home to me unharmed."

Gerard remembered the basics of how to bow to royalty and managed not to embarrass himself too badly executing it. Newt went to one knee, his shaggy head bent for the barest moment before he was back on his feet.

The queen did not seem to take offense, either at Gerard's clumsiness or Newt's brevity.

Sir Caedor looked expectant for a moment, before a glower settled on his face. Guinevere must have sensed that because she turned back to him, reached up into her hair, and pulled out one of the silver pins holding the coil in place. She raised one delicately arched eyebrow at the knight until he lifted his hand so that she could place the pin into his gauntleted palm and closed his fingers over it.

"And for you, brave protector, a token of my own. Bring these boys, so dear to my lord and husband, back home safe."

"As God is my witness, madam."

And with that, Guinevere turned and departed, leaving only the sound of the horses shifting and chomping at their bits and the muted murmuring of the servants.

"Well, I had hoped to be able to send you directly to wherever she's taken the girl," Merlin said, filling the gap in the conversation. The three travelers winced at the thought of being transported magically into an unknown situation, but Merlin went on as though he hadn't noticed. "Unfortunately, Morgain has covered her tracks far too well. It is some small consolation that my wards have held up and that she could not scry into Camelot but had to risk coming here herself to spy."

"A pity she uses her skills in such unwomanly ways as to challenge her lord and brother," Sir Caedor said.

Once, Gerard would have agreed with the knight. Having faced off against the sorceress before, and having looked into her eyes as she faced defeat not with fear but dignity and pride, he was no longer so quick to condemn. Morgain was an outsider, and by nature of her gender deemed unfit to use her talents to do more than maintain her own household, or support her brother Arthur's goals. That seemed unfair, somehow.

Yes, she was a woman. But she was also powerful—a strong warrior with unusual skills, second only to Merlin himself. Could there not have been some way to make use of her; to make her into an ally, rather than a foe? If so, that moment was long gone.

And if Ailis did have magical abilities, the way Merlin believed she did, Gerard hoped for her sake that they were not as strong. She would doubtless be happier that way. He would not wish Merlin's isolation, nor Morgain's bitterness, on her, ever.

"But you will not have to ride the entire way," Merlin continued. "I'm not so far in my dotage as that. I shall set you on your way with a bit of a . . . hmmm . . . let us call it a push. And I will grant you some aid once you arrive.

"Here." Merlin handed Gerard a small object. "Since Morgain is so inconsiderately capable at warding herself, you'll have to do things the difficult way. By sneaking in."

Gerard looked at the object Merlin had given him, then held it up by the leather thong wrapped around it.

It looked like an ordinary river-stone; gray, smooth, and flat, about the size of Gerard's palm, rounder at one end and narrow at the other, almost like a teardrop. The rawhide strap was strung through a neatly bored hole at the narrowed end and tied off, creating a loop long enough to hang over one's neck. With a glance at Merlin for confirmation, Gerard put it around his neck.

"A stone?" Sir Caedor asked.

"A lodestone," Merlin said. "A lodestone containing a hair from the missing girl-child and a drop of my own blood, among other things you need not worry about. It will lead you to her by the swiftest means available to you, like a pigeon flying back to its cote. I strongly suspect that Morgain has gone to ground in the Orkneys, her mother's home. She is well-known there, and will feel protected by that. It is a rough land, full of tough-minded folk, but keep to the lodestone and let nothing deter you."

Merlin looked at Sir Caedor. "That is where your companion comes in. My good sir . . ." and Merlin put a rounded, rich tone into his voice that made the knight's shoulders go back and his chest puff out almost instinctively. "Good sir, King Arthur himself places these lads into your care and protection. They have a mission to accomplish that none other might manage, not only to rescue the girl-child, but to learn in doing so what the sorceress Morgain plans next. Upon you, then, rests the responsibility of getting them to their destination intact, and in time to do what they must do."

Gerard realized that he had underestimated Merlin once again. The enchanter was still danger-ously short-tempered and rude, with a wicked sense of humor that most did not appreciate, but he also knew how to coax people when his other tools would not work. And he was very, very good at it.

"Right, then," Merlin said, stepping back from the trio as they remounted their horses. "As Sir Caedor has urged, time is fleeing. Off you go. And boys"—Merlin caught their gazes—"remember to trust your instincts. What you have inside you is more important than what you may see outside. Remember that!"

"We will," Newt said. Gerard nodded solemnly, reaching down to take Merlin's hand in his own. The enchanter seemed somewhat surprised by the action, but returned the clasp firmly, his hand as hard and strong as any knight's.

"Go. And may the gods, old and new, be with you."

Gerard turned his mount to face the arched exit. Newt fell in close behind on Loyal, and the mule was tied by a lead rope to his saddle, leaving Sir Caedor to take up the rear.

Merlin raised his arms and chanted something that was caught up in the sudden wind. Gerard shook the hair out of his eyes and squinted, watching the space in front of them. He could hear Newt muttering to Loyal, keeping his mount calm while the portal formed.

When the circular hole in time and space was complete, Gerard took a deep breath and put his heels to his horse's flanks. Sir Caedor and Newt did likewise, and they rode through the portal, out of Camelot, and once more into the unknown.

SEVEN

There were waves crashing outside, white-capped waters dashing into and around the rocky cliff. Ailis could see them from the window of her room. This was not the same place where they had confronted Morgain before, on the Isle of Apples, although it did seem to be an island. From the coast-line she could see in the near distance and the heavy tang of salt in the air, Ailis suspected that she was in the Orkneys, in the castle of Morgain's—and Arthur's—birth; the one place where Arthur had given Morgain sole rule, as the daughter of their mother, Ingraine of Orkney.

That was all Ailis knew from the gossip that flew around Camelot. She had never cared nor had a reason to learn more before encountering Morgain in person. And afterward, there had been no one she felt comfortable enough to ask.

When she had finally woke completely, the same servant from before had been waiting for her. Ailis's eyes were clearer, but the woman still seemed not to be solid around the edges, as though she wasn't quite entirely there. Ailis had decided that she didn't want to think about it too much and focused instead on the warm robe and deerskin slippers that were offered.

The fact that she was now Morgain's captive had filled her mind, driving everything else out. Morgain, the sorceress. Morgain, who had reason to hate her. Morgain the cruel . . . the evil . . . the merciless.

Play meek, her common sense told her. *Play mild. Be the good, gentle maid. Morgain won't do anything to you if you don't provoke her.*

Once dressed, she had been escorted by the servant from a small room to a much larger one. It held a bed, a wardrobe, and a small desk with writing implements, as though she were free to write a letter to anyone. There was a window large enough for her to climb through—though so far above the rocky ground that to attempt it would be certain death.

The servant had given her a warning: "Do not try to escape, or dire things will happen, child," and had left her to her own devices. That had been, as far as she could tell, two days ago. The sun had moved across the overcast sky and set, the night stars had glowed and faded, and the sun had risen again. Food was delivered at regular intervals, morning and evening, brought in on a small silver cart that moved as though pushed by invisible hands. Ailis ate, and ate well, and then the silver cart went away, her chamber doors opening for it without hesitation.

Meek. Mild. Well-behaved. Taking the servant's warning to heart, Ailis tried to keep herself busy within those four walls; tried not to think about what might be awaiting her. She counted the stone blocks in the walls. She counted the oval tiles around the window. She tried to create recognizable shapes out of the shadows the candles cast around her. She recited to herself every poem she had ever heard a love-struck courtier utter, and all the scraps of songs and stories she could recall.

Even before she had ridden out with Gerard and Newt, patience had not been a strength of hers, and boredom had overcome her fear by the end of the first day. After pacing back and forth in front of the door all morning, Ailis found herself reaching for the latch. It turned easily, opening into a larger room, this one with a fireplace, a soft couch, and a thick white fur rug on the floor from some impossibly huge beast. The fireplace was laid with wood that lit itself when she said she was cold, and extinguished itself when she told it she was warm enough now, thank you.

That discovery occupied her for the course of one evening. She justified herself by saying that she was still staying where she had been placed. Would the room be furnished if she were not meant to use it? Would the fireplace have been laid and ready for her, if she was not meant to warm herself in front of it?

* * *

The next morning, she grew restless quickly. Ailis paced the confines of the two rooms, stopping only to eat the meals brought to her and to take a bath in the small tub filled with warm water that appeared by the fireplace, fresh white towels piled beside it.

Clean, well-fed, and totally without anything to do for the first time in her life, Ailis thought she might scream. Meek and mild had *never* been her— not even when she was a servant. But you did what you needed to do to survive.

"I'm bored," she told the room, as though the magic that brought meals and fire might bring entertainment as well. But nothing happened.

Finally, something inside Ailis snapped and she could not take one more hour of those same walls, that same view. She dressed in the warm wool garments she found in the wardrobe, combed and braided her hair into one thick red plait that fell halfway down her back, put the warm slippers back on, and opened the one door she had not yet tried—the one that led to the rest of the castle.

"This isn't the wisest thing you've ever done," she told herself. "But it's better than growing any older waiting in that room."

Like Camelot, the halls were made of stone, cut into blocks and mortared together. Unlike Camelot, the stone of the floor was covered with a narrow carpet that ran down the center of the hall as far as she could see. The carpet was midnight blue, with intricate patterns in dark reds and traces of silver thread, and was surprisingly soft to her hand. Ailis could not even begin to imagine how expensive such a carpet must be, to be placed on the floor where anyone might tread on it, rather than hanging on the wall where she was used to seeing them.

The stone of the walls was smooth-textured, cream-colored, and lit by sconces set into it. The dark yellow candles inside burned brightly, without any smoke or soot, and gave off a delicate odor of wax. There were a few other doors along the hallway similar to hers, but she chose not to try any of them. Instead, she went to the end of the hall and pushed open a pair of heavy, carved doors.

"Rrrrrrrr . . ."

Startled by the sound, Ailis almost turned on her heels and ran, but the thought that it might be better to be eaten by a beast than die of boredom in that room kept her where she was.

"Rrrrrrrr?"

The noise changed from threatening to inquisitive, and she was able to slow her heartbeat enough to actually look at the creature confronting her.

It was the size of a plow horse, but no horse had ever been so fabulous. The head was that of a great hawk, black eyes shaded by a tuft of golden-yellow feathers, the cruelly curved beak dark as jet. But instead of a bird's body, the hawk's head was attached to the crouching form of a great cat, the tail lashing back and forth tufted not with fur, but a clutch of small golden feathers.

Ailis walked around the beast, carefully keeping her distance. The hawk's head turned to follow her movements, its tail slowing its movement as the creature went from surprised hostility to curiosity.

She wished that Newt were there with her. He grew up with beasts—dogs and horses, admittedly. But he dealt well with the dragon they had encountered, under that same beastish logic. And that dragon had been a thinking, speaking creature!

"Do you . . . can you speak?" she asked it. Best to be polite, rather than risk offending a creature that could tear her flesh with one pounce. The great clawed forepaws twitched, but the creature did not make another noise.

"That might be a no, then. Or it might be that you're choosing not to speak. Which is it?"

The beast shifted to follow her movements, and Ailis jumped back, stumbling and hitting her shoulder against the wall in her surprise. Not because the creature moved, but because of what that movement revealed.

Wings. Great, thick-feathered wings, folded against the plush fur of its body.

"Aren't you lovely!" she exclaimed.

"Rrrrrr?" Ailis took the sound to mean that although the beast might not be able to speak with its beak, it understood her words. Or at least her intentions.

"Such a lovely creature," she said, keeping her voice modulated normally, not resorting to the high-pitched tones some of the ladies of the court used when speaking to their lapdogs. Those whines annoyed her, and she couldn't imagine it wouldn't annoy a creature with the acute hearing of a bird.

"May I pet you? I promise not to muss your feathers."

The beast watched her, then lowered its head to the floor, resting its beak on the carpet. One eye kept watch on Ailis but the gesture seemed a clear invitation, so she took a step closer, then another, until she was close enough to reach out and touch the golden pelt.

The fur was thick and rougher than she had been expecting, but warm and pliant, the muscles underneath flexing and relaxing under her touch.

"Oh, you are *such* a lovely. Are there any others like you? I have heard of dragons and bridge trolls, and everyone has heard of unicorns, of course. But I've never heard of anything like you."

And then she noticed it at the same moment she felt it vibrating under her hand. A massive purr rumbled up from deep within the creature. Delighted laughter filled her throat and for the first time in days, perhaps weeks, Ailis felt totally relaxed and happy.

"Are you magic?" she asked it. "Of course you must be; you're a magical beast. But are you magic to cause such happiness with such a simple sound?"

The beast sighed, shifting slightly as though to lean more into her touch, and kept purring.

"No, I can't stay here all day and pet you, silly thing."

Why not? a small voice in her head asked; not the voice she had become somewhat used to hearing, of Merlin giving advice. But a more familiar one—of self-doubt and second-guessing. Why shouldn't she stay here? Surely they could not call this an attempt to escape, not if she was found with a beast clearly belonging to Morgain. And it would be difficult to feel bored or trapped in the company of such a happy purr. *And think of how much you would enjoy telling Newt about it. He would be so jealous, not to have met—*

And that thought stopped any inclination to stay put. How could she tell Newt anything while trapped in Morgain's castle? No one knew where she was or who had taken her, or that Morgain had been inside Camelot to start with. Nobody would be coming to save her. If she wanted to do more than grow old inside her gilded cage then she had to find answers for herself.

"I'm sorry, lovely. But I have to go."

She stepped away, watching carefully to make sure that the beast did not take offense, and looked around to explore more of the chamber they were in. It was a round room with high ceilings, and three sets of wooden doors; the ones she had come through were carved with dragons, the ones to her left had sleek cats entwined in play, and the ones to her right had flames wrapped around twined roses.

Neither of the two new sets of doors gave her a clue as to where to go.

"Any suggestions, my friend?" she asked, not expecting an answer, and therefore not disappointed when none came.

Merlin? she asked inside her head. *Do you have any suggestions for me? Now would be a good time.*

She hadn't expected an answer from the enchanter, either. Not here inside Morgain's own home. But the silence in her head felt lonely nonetheless.

"That one, then," she decided, purely on impulse, and pushed through the carved doors.

* * *

"She's a brave one, that's for certain," Morgain said to herself, watching the girl move on down the hallway. The griffin perked up, as though it had somehow heard her words, and seemed to look directly into the scrying crystal Morgain was using to observe her unwilling guest.

"Yes, all right," Morgain said in response to the unspoken question posed by her pet. "Go on, then."

Given permission, the beast got to its feet and, with an agility natural to its cat body, turned to follow Ailis through the doors.

"Interesting," Morgain said to herself, a smile curving her bloodred lips, giving a softer cast to her face.

The sound of the door opening behind her caused her to curl her fingers over the crystal, blanking out the scene she had been watching. Only one person would dare intrude upon her, and she had no intention of sharing everything that went on in her home with that individual.

When she turned to greet the uninvited guest, the smile on her face had changed to a warmer but less sincere one.

"It is customary to knock," she said lightly, nothing in her tone or posture showing her anger, "when entering your host's private study."

"We have gone beyond politeness, you and I," the figure said. Wrapped in a heavy gray cloak, despite the warmth of the room, the speaker poured a glass of deep red wine from the bottle waiting on a small table, then sank into an ornately carved wooden chair and looked sideways at Morgain. "We have no time for your little games right now. There are more important things to deal with. Your brother has taken the bait we set for him."

"As I knew he would," Morgain said with satisfaction. "Using the Marcher Lords' pride was a brilliant stroke. No king worth his salt dares ignore unrest along his borders." She settled in her own seat and smoothed the fabric of her dress before looking up again, her eyes intent. "Tell me more."

EIGHT

"Oh. My. Lord."

Newt was too busy throwing up to care about the misery in Sir Caedor's voice. The moment they had trotted through Merlin's gateway, he had slipped from Loyal's back, landing on his hands and knees in the grass. He puked up the oatcakes and hot tea he'd had for breakfast.

"That's . . . never happened before." Like Gerard had been through so many portals, to be such an expert, Newt thought with what energy he could spare.

"Hush, pup," Sir Caedor said, clearly echoing Newt's own thoughts. The knight was leaning against his own mare, one hand curled around his stirrup-cup as though needing it to remain upright. Gerard alone remained on his horse's back, but he was leaning forward against its neck, clenching the mane between his fingers, his complexion pale. Giving up, he slid with a groan down onto the grass behind Newt and rested his face against the cool earth.

Newt stopped heaving, set back on his heels, and wiped his mouth with the back of his sleeve. Water. He needed water to wash his mouth out. He got to his feet slowly, unsteadily, and turned to remove a waterskin from its tie-down on Loyal's saddle. What he saw, over the horse's withers, made him forget all about his recent incapacitation.

Black clouds scudded across the sky, ominous roiling shapes gathering over distant hilltops, moving far too fast to be anything other than a rainstorm—a very bad rainstorm.

"I think we've hit a patch of bad weather," Newt said, trying to sound casual. "Any idea if there's shelter nearby?"

"The blighted wizard's thrown us near three or four days' riding upland," Sir Caedor said, looking around before raising his eyes to the incoming storm. "Well past Londinium and the worst of the Cotswold Hills."

Gerard was still on the ground, now looking decidedly green. "I don't think I can ride."

"Then we're going to get very wet."

"Over there," Sir Caedor said, recovering faster than either one of them. He gestured toward a low rise of grass, with a notable overhang facing them. "Come on, lad, get up. You can make it over there."

"I . . ."

"Get *up*, boy. *Now*." His voice was tough, but not unkind. With a combination of encouraging words and a strong hand, Sir Caedor got Gerard back on his feet, and the three began walking as swiftly as they could, not willing to get back on their horses until the dizziness of the magical transport subsided.

"Umm . . ." Newt said as they got close enough to see the overhang better. The rise was perhaps twice Sir Caedor's height, and several man-lengths long, with enough room to shelter all three of them and at least two of the animals.

"It's the only thing around, boy." Sir Caedor was clearly impatient at Newt's hesitation. Even Gerard looked at him sideways when the stable boy dug his heels in. The horses continued forward, but the mule also stopped, its ears twitching in agitation.

"That's a barrow: a giant grave, a resting place for the bones of great warriors from an earlier time, built into the turf."

"It's shelter. The dead won't mind."

"The dead *always* mind," Newt said, but allowed himself to be coaxed forward, dragging the mule along in turn. Neither of them looked happy about it.

Gerard and Sir Caedor were two stones from the same quarry, Newt thought ruefully; it didn't occur to them that disturbing the dead, even the long-dead, never led to anything good. Stubborn, headstrong, ignorant warriors, both of them, so certain that nothing in the ground could be a threat.

He hoped that they were right.

The barrow was smaller than they'd thought, so they unsaddled the horses and took the packs off the mule. They shoved the packs as far under the overhang as they could just as the air darkened around them, going from clear morning light to shadowed dusk instantly with the arrival of the storm clouds.

"I hate storms," Sir Caedor muttered. "All inconvenience, no redeeming value."

"Grows the crops," Gerard said.

"Hmmmph." The knight removed his armor and fit as much of himself under the overhang as he could, his legs sticking out into the open air. Gerard sat next to him, his legs tucked up underneath.

"Newt, leave them. They know about storms."

"It's not the storms I'm worried about," Newt muttered again, but not loud enough for either of them to hear. He finished tethering the horses to a running line, gave the mule a comforting pat on the side, and came to join the other two.

"This reminds me of a time during my early years, when I was still trying to make my name . . ." Sir Caedor began, and while Newt didn't bother to look interested, Gerard settled in to hear the man's story. At the very least, it would be a way to pass the time while they waited for the storm to pass.

Halfway into Caedor's somewhat disjointed and rambling tale of a long-forgotten battle in the highlands, a downward strike of lightning startled the horses, making them shift and shudder uneasily.

"Here comes the rain," Gerard said needlessly, as a wave of water came down in sharp pellets. "Hopefully it won't last long. Merlin gave us a gift, sending us this far along. I'd hate to waste it."

Sir Caedor grunted, clearly annoyed at how nature had taken the steam out of his story. Newt merely shifted on the ground, feeling a cold prickle on the back of his neck that had nothing to do with the air turning colder.

"We shouldn't be here."

"No, we should be back at Camelot, warm and dry," Sir Caedor said. "But that's not the lot of a knight, and we do not complain. The lot of a knight is to champion his king, and complete his mission no matter the cost."

But Newt had stopped listening to the knight.

"Something's spooking the horses," he said, watching them shift and look over their shoulders out into the driving rain.

"More than the storm?" Gerard asked. He might be leading this journey, but when it came to livestock, he deferred to Newt's experience.

"I think so."

"There is nothing out there save a few sodden rabbits," Sir Caedor said, dismissing Newt's fears. "As I was saying, this reminds me of when I was a young knight, out to—"

Newt got to his feet and walked slowly out into the rain, his hand resting lightly on the dagger he kept strapped to his upper leg.

"Be careful," Gerard said, picking up on Newt's unease.

The ground squished under Newt's feet, all grass and mud. His balance was thrown off by the slippery surface, and when he reached the first horse, he laid one hand on the beast's flank to steady himself while he tried to wipe the waterlogged hair out of his eyes in order to see better.

"Newt?"

"I don't know. I think—" He got no further before the ground seemed to rise up to assault him, a hard slap across his face pushed him away from the horse, causing him to stagger and fall on his backside. The mud splashed up around him, getting in his mouth and eyes, but not so much that he couldn't see his attackers coming forward through the rain: tall, elongated, with narrow, sharp-chinned faces; mouths too wide; eyes oddly shaped. Narrow hands reached for him, mud dripping off to reveal white bones underneath.

"Barrow-wights!" Newt yelped, scrabbling backward toward the overhang. Realizing that it would be no safer there, he crawled forward just as quickly.

"Look out!" Gerard yelled, dashing forward as another figure rose out of the dirt, coming toward Newt. The horses stamped their hooves and snorted, clearly wanting to run away, but restrained by the tie-downs.

"Sir Caedor, help me!" Gerard shouted, knocking up against one of the mud-covered figures and coming away with only a handful of mud to show for it. His sword did no damage at all, as far as he could tell. The wight slashed at him, scoring him on the same cheek Merlin had cut. Unlike Merlin's blade, this slice stung like fire. He might not be able to hurt them, but they could clearly hurt him.

"Sir Caedor!" he called again, more urgently this time. The knight, his sword drawn, took a pair of wights down with one blow, but found himself surrounded again almost immediately.

"We need to get away from here!" Newt said, somehow getting to his feet and fumbling with the knots he had recently tied in his horse's reins. The water had already swollen the leather to the point where the knots were almost impossible to undo. In desperation, he swiped at them with his dagger, cutting the horses loose and grabbing at the now-flapping reins before they could bolt.

"Our supplies!" Sir Caedor said, reaching back underneath to grab the closest pack. "Squire, distract them!"

"Distract?" Gerard asked in disbelief, then turned to face the mud-covered skeletons once again. "Right. Distract." Lifting his sword and holding it lengthwise across his body like a barrier, he charged the nearest wights—four of them now, and more shaking free of the ground even as he moved—screaming at the top of his lungs: "Arthur! The Pendragon! Camelot!"

By now covered with mud from the number of times he had slipped and fallen, Newt was worried that Gerard might attack him, as well. Using the horses as cover, he reached out to grab the first pack from Sir Caedor, slinging it over his mud- and rain-slicked shoulder. He shoved one foot into Loyal's stirrup, and swung up into the saddle. He pushed the horse forward, using the beast's bulk to knock over one of the wights. It fell, while striking out with one bony hand at the horse's eyes.

"Sir Caedor, here!" He shoved the reins of one horse into the knight's hands, not waiting to see what the older man did with them. He was a knight; he knew how to handle himself in battle. Kicking his horse forward again, Newt moved away from the barrow and into the melee of Gerard and six—no, seven mud-coated wights. "Ger! Up!"

The squire risked a look away, saw the third horse, and dove for the saddle, dragging himself up into it by sheer force of will.

The moment Gerard was secure in the saddle,

Newt urged both horses into a full-out run, not bothering to check and see if Sir Caedor and the rest of the supplies were with them. From the thundering of hooves hard on their heels, the knight had wasted no time following their lead.

The barrow-wights, having driven the intruders away from their resting place, did not bother to follow.

NINE

The morning of the fifth day after her abduction, Ailis woke in her comfortable bed and stretched, feeling not fear or boredom, but anticipation. For the first time in her life, the first time she could remember, there were no chores in front of her; no duties, no responsibilities. Nothing except what she might find in the course of her explorations.

It had taken her a while to get over her fear that someone would drag her back to her rooms and punish her for leaving. But this morning those fears seemed as far away as . . . Camelot.

After a quick sponge bath in front of the fireplace in her sitting room, she dressed in the comfortable clothing unseen servants had left for her the night before: a durable russet wool dress that matched her hair color, worn over a cream-colored shift of some soft material that moved against her skin as though it were alive, and her now-familiar deerskin slippers. She supposed that the slippers on her feet were a reminder that she was not to leave the castle, while the clothing—otherwise suited for exploring—was tacit permission to continue as she was going.

But regardless of the clothing's purpose, there was no possible way Ailis could stay in her room. Not when she had discovered such magical wonders waiting for her in the seemingly endless hallways of this place!

"Rrrrrrrr?"

The griffin's greeting had become an expected part of her morning. Ailis pushed through the wooden doors and walked confidently over to scratch its lowered head, just behind where ears might be on another beast.

"Good morning to you, too, Sir Tawny." She had not been able to come up with a name that conveyed the combination of dignity and affection the beast showed her, and so fell back on a descriptive nickname, the way her family had once called her Red. "Are you ready to go?"

She had been surprised on the first day when the griffin had decided to follow her—surprised but strangely comforted. At the same time, she was not at all surprised that every passage she wandered down in the seemingly endless maze of halls, and every room she chose to go into, was large enough for the creature to go with her, save her bedchamber. When she returned to her rooms, the beast waited in the hallway until she was safely inside, and then disappeared back to whatever lair he slept in.

"Are you guard or guest?" she had wondered. Yet there was no reply beyond a black-eyed blink and a low rumbling purr.

Now Sir Tawny followed her wherever she went, and if Ailis was disappointed to encounter no other living thing in her rambles, the things she did discover more than made up for it.

Today she was returning to the hall of colors. As best she could tell, it was in the center of the keep. The ceiling was arched with great soaring beams, and between those beams, rather than wood or stone, glass separated inside from out—colored glass, blues and greens, shading from dark to light the way an ocean might if you were to see it from below the water's surface.

When you stood in the middle of the hall and looked up, you *were* under the surface of the ocean.

Great fish swam by, huge-finned things with sharp teeth, elongated creatures with silvery shells and dark red eyes, massive schools of tiny glittering fish that turned and turned again almost more quickly than her eye could follow.

None of it was real. She knew that. But it was so lovely, so solid-looking, that even Sir Tawny tried to take a bite out of a passing fish.

"Do you think Morgain wishes she were able to live underwater? Is that why she created this? Do you think she's actually *been* under the ocean?" Anything was possible to one with as much magic as the sorceress.

Ailis stood watching the magical illusions float past, and could almost imagine that she herself was underwater, breathing as fish do. Her arms rose, and she moved them the way she might in a pond or lake. Her eyes closed, and the fish began to gather around her, as though drawn by her efforts. One of them brushed by her cheek, and the contact made her giggle. That in turn made her open her eyes again, and she stared into the gullet of a huge fish, four times her own size, toothy mouth open as though it were about to swallow her whole.

Ailis screamed, jumped back, and fell, landing

on her backside on the floor. Her eyes went wide, and she spread her fingers as though searching for a rock or stick or anything that might be used as a weapon to fend this monster off. Her heart sped up to the point where she couldn't hear anything except a thumping in her chest. The air suddenly felt cold and clammy against her skin.

"Sir Tawny?" she managed to croak out, but the griffin did not come to her rescue. She could not take her eyes off the sea monster long enough to look around for him.

No way to tell herself that this was all magic; that the fish could not really truly exist; that they were on solid ground, not deep in the ocean. Those teeth looked far too real, too solid. And magic could kill just as easily as an ordinary sword. All it took was intent.

Don't be some fish's meal, Ailis. . . . Merlin? A faint whisper, barely even there. She probably imagined it. No matter. She grabbed onto it, angry at the thought that the enchanter might think she would be so weak, to be taken down by a figment of magic. . . .

"Not me! No you don't!" she cried, throwing up her arms and closing her eyes again as the monster loomed closer, rancid breath blowing onto her skin and up her nose. The smell made her want to gag. She was overcome with disgust, swamping even the fear until all she felt was revulsion, and from that revulsion came more anger. "Get. Away. From. Me!"

A blast of fish-gut breath washed over her and . . . then it was gone.

Ailis opened her eyes to an empty chamber. Even the colors seemed more muted now, tinted with a pale golden light rather than the watery green of earlier.

"Rrrrr?"

Shaking so badly she could hardly take it, Ailis reached out and found a handful of warm feathers, and the cool breath of the griffin reached over her like a benediction.

"Some help you were," she said, using him to haul herself up off the floor. She looked around the room and shuddered.

"I almost forgot," she said. "It's pretty, but it's still magic. *Morgain's* magic. Nothing good can come from that." It had been nice while it lasted, that feeling of freedom—of pleasure without price—but it was a dream, and she was awake now. Something inside her protested, but the weight of her terror, and the knowledge that nobody would save her if she could not save herself, weighed down that ambition until it sank without a trace. Ailis was a practical girl. She'd always had to be: no room for dreams in the life of a servant. That was what had saved her over and over again. It would be what saved her again now, if anything did.

She thought about going back to her room and locking the door behind her, but that didn't seem right, either. Hiding was easy, but not always practical.

"I need to find a way out of here," she said. "I can't stay. I can't let the dream make me forget." There was more at stake here than just her own comfort. Morgain had found her way into Camelot's walls, and only Ailis knew. That meant that Camelot was in danger, terrible danger. She had to tell Merlin—or tell the king. She had to tell someone, somehow.

Sir Tawny sighed in disappointment, but otherwise remained silent.

* * *

"Wise girl," Morgain murmured, passing her hand over her scrying mirror and making the image of the two figures disappear. "Wise, wise girl." She did not know whether to be annoyed or amused by the witch-child, who had so far refused to succumb to her fears, despite being completely out of her element.

It was tempting to go to that floor, to walk with the witch-child and show her the wonders hidden therein; to teach her how to control the seascape room so that the shark would attack at her command; explain the proper way to make the wall-lights glow according to your mood; or shift the puzzle-floor so that the creatures depicted in the mosaic underfoot seemed to gambol and dance.

She could not let the girl go. Morgain considered that she could have easily killed Ailis the moment she realized someone had seen her in Camelot's halls. She had in fact planned on it at first. But then Morgain recognized the face, those dark eyes filled with horror and surprise but no hatred. Something had made her take the girl instead—take her and keep her.

She supposed the thought had been there from the beginning: No child so filled with the potential for magic should be left untutored. Merlin had seen it and had clearly put his touch on her . . . but he had not taken her as a student, the foolish old man. So Ailis was still fair game.

Morgain didn't want a student, herself. Too much effort, too much bother. But a hostage—one with potential to be useful in the long run . . . that was a different matter.

And so the girl was being treated more as an honored guest than a prisoner. No prisoner ever had such run of this place before—not even prisoners who *thought* they were honored guests. Morgain felt a twinge of regret at her actions, but she stifled it firmly. There were other brands in the fire, other considerations to be . . . considered.

There were others in residence who must be kept in mind. Others who would not be pleased to know of the girl's existence.

And yet, how much harm could it do, to speak with the girl—to allay her fears, perhaps, and prevent any unfortunate and doomed attempt to escape? The process of winning her over, making her more pliable, more . . . useful had begun.

Yes, Morgain decided, reaching down to stroke the ears of the great black cat sleeping by her side. She would do just that—for the girl's own good, and her own as well.

*　*　*

"Here? You intend for us to camp here?"

Gerard looked around in confusion at the

knight's outburst. Newt had chosen a good spot to make camp: a flat clearing a short distance off the wide dirt track they had been riding on. Surrounded on two sides by thick-trunked oak trees, with a small creek running along the third side, it seemed a pleasant enough place to stop. There was wood for the fire, water for cooking and drinking, grass for the horses to graze on, and it was far enough from the road that if travelers went by during the night, they would not be seen. In fact, Gerard had been about to compliment Newt on his scouting, as soon as he got back from watering the horses downstream.

"What is wrong with it, sir?" Gerard asked politely. His face might hurt from the strain, but he was polite. King Arthur and Sir Rheynold would expect no less from him.

Sir Caedor went off into a litany of things that were wrong with their campsite, most of which seemed to revolve around the fact that they would be sleeping outside on blankets, rather than inside on beds. Sir Caedor, it appeared, did not enjoy being outside of walls at night, especially this far north of Camelot's reach, among people he deemed "savages and heathens."

Gerard added all this to the list of things that Sir

Caedor did not like, which so far included the way the mule had been loaded, the pace they were traveling at—too slowly, consulting the lodestone too often rather than simply aiming themselves in the general direction it indicated—the dried foods they had brought, the way that the boys did almost everything, and Newt, on principle. Newt himself had obviously been holding back laughter at some of the knight's comments about "lowly brats" and "the stench of stable," but Gerard was considering notions of how to teach the older man some manners.

"I've heard worse," Newt told him. "From you, in fact."

Gerard had to admit the truth of that. They had not gotten off to a good start. Their first meeting involved an exchange of insults, a fistfight, and a scolding from Sir Lancelot. But Newt had proven himself since then. He had become a friend.

None of this seemed to matter to Sir Caedor. When they had stopped to water their horses around mid-afternoon on the first day, Caedor had handed his reins to Newt and gone off to the bushes in order to relieve himself, saying over his shoulder only that Gerard should make sure that "that boy" did not take anything from his saddlebag. Yes, Newt did work in the stables, but Caedor's casual lack of respect—due even a kitchen scullion—had made Gerard's jaw drop in astonishment. This was not how he had been taught that a knight should behave. It was certainly not how the men who trained him would act, not even when they were in their cups during a long-running banquet, or exhausted after a hard-won tourney.

If it had been up to him, Gerard would have mounted and ridden away right then, leaving Sir Caedor's horse tied to an old oak tree. Newt, however, had merely shrugged and picked up Gerard's reins as well. "It's not worth it. He is who he is. And all he sees when he looks at me is the stables. That's never going to change."

"It's not fair."

"You're still on about fairness?" Newt made a noise like a horse's snort. "Grow up, Ger."

"You shouldn't take that sort of—"

"Gerard, he's a knight. Annoying, yes, but no better or worse than anyone else." Newt looked at the squire with a sort of pity. "You need to stop thinking of them as if they're made of gold. They're men, that's all. Men who are very good with weapons, good on horseback, but . . ."

"We take a vow when we're knighted," Gerard protested.

"You haven't taken the vow yet, and you're a good fellow. Someone who isn't . . . how is a vow of charity, chastity, and honor going to create something that isn't there?"

"You're wrong. Being a knight *means* something."

"To you it does," Newt allowed.

Gerard drew breath dramatically to retort, but a voice in the back of his head suggested that carrying on would be pointless. Gerard reached up to rub at the wound Merlin had left on his face, which still itched, and let the discussion go.

They waited in silence for the knight, then remounted and moved on.

And yet those words from hours past had been a heavy weight in Gerard's throat since then, until he felt as though he were going to choke on it. He needed to show respect for the older man, and yet he also needed to respect the training they had both sworn to live by.

Oblivious of where Gerard's thoughts had taken him, the knight was still talking. "All that aside, no matter that it might be the perfect location, it might indeed be the best campsite in all of Britain. But servants should serve, not make decisions."

That was it. That was just *it*. Gerard had tried to heed Merlin's words. Had tried to be polite. Had tried to hold on to the last scraps of his patience and tolerance, and respect that a knight of Sir Caedor's years and experience deserved, no matter how he behaved now. But nobody insulted Newt except Gerard. He rubbed again at the wound and spoke his mind.

"We *all* serve. We were sent on this journey by our king. A journey, in accordance with the code of the Round Table, to protect and defend a damsel in need—a person under Camelot's protection, threatened by one of Camelot's foes." It was as though Sir Rheynold—or even Arthur himself—had taken over Gerard's mouth, speaking with his tongue. The emotion behind the words, though, was his own. He believed in the code of chivalry, the idea that the stronger protect the weaker. He believed in it with a passion that fueled everything he did, everything he was—everything he wanted to be.

Sir Caedor had the grace to look down, in shame, hearing that reminder of their responsibilities and obligations.

"As to your comments about Newt, you might wish to reconsider them as well," Gerard went on. "We are traveling light, as you yourself have noted. No tents. No pavilions. No servants to fetch and carry for us. Despite what you may think of Newt, on this he is an equal to me and to you. *Not* a servant or stable boy."

That brought the knight's head back up, his cheeks burning with anger. "You dare speak so to me?"

Gerard was quaking in his saddle, actually terrified at what he was saying—and to whom. Still, the point needed to be driven home, no matter the cost. "I have no choice, Sir Caedor. This must be said."

The knight took a deep breath, ran one hand over his thick ruff of graying hair, and stared off into the distance. His face was seamed and heavy with age, and his mouth was turned down in a frown. But he was hearing what Gerard had said. Hearing, and thinking. Gerard went on.

"If we had passed an inn last night, or tonight, or any other night, we would have stayed there." They had to rest, and given the choice between dirt and a bed, not even Newt would choose dirt. "Have you seen any inns along the way?" Gerard asked.

Sir Caedor now looked thunderous. "No."

"And do you know of any in the near distance that we could arrive at before dark?" Gerard knew that he was pushing his luck, but Sir Rheynold had always taught him that you needed to establish control the first time someone questioned your authority, not the sixth or seventh time. By then it was too late and your weakness was known. *Arthur, your wisdom, please. Merlin, your cunning. Now would be a good time for the spell to kick in. . . .*

"There are no inns around this part of the countryside," Sir Caedor said, spitting out each word as though it were bitter. "It's a desolate, godforsaken land. I know this. I fought here during the battle of Traeth Tryfrwyd."

Gerard looked around, as much to avoid yet another story of Sir Caedor's "glorious past" as to figure out what the knight was talking about now.

Sir Caedor had a point. The lands around Camelot were fertile, even where rocky, and the trees were tall, strong things. The farther north they had traveled, fewer things grew, either cultivated or otherwise. Their destination would be, Sir Caedor claimed, even more stark; islands of barren rocks and dry soil, with nothing to recommend it, save access to the seas and a reputation for fierce fighters.

"Yes, it is barren," Gerard agreed. "And this is the best place we saw for making camp."

Sir Caedor did not respond.

Gerard took the silence as tacit compliance. He raised a hand as though to officially end the conversation, then turned and walked down to the creek, meeting Newt as he came back with the horses on lead ropes, the mule trailing behind on its own.

"The water cold?"

Newt shook his head, his wet hair spraying drops into Gerard's face, as intended. "Cold enough. You should bathe, too. You're getting somewhat ripe under there."

Newt had declined the offer of leather chest and leg protection like the ones that Gerard wore, claiming that it would slow him down if it came time to fight or run. When the sweat began to form under the padding, sticking to his skin until it itched, Sir Caedor's armor had to be even more uncomfortable. Gerard thought that maybe the stable boy was the wisest of the three of them.

"Perhaps in the morning, when the sun's come up again." He didn't have the distrust of bathing that many of the knights and squires had, but it seemed foolish to tempt fate by getting himself wet in the cool air.

"Sir Caedor taking care of dinner?"

Gerard let out a surprised laugh. Newt and Ailis had always managed to do that; to make him laugh, even when he didn't want to. "Somehow, I don't think so. You want to wrestle for the job?"

"Nah, you can do it."

"Oh, thank you."

"Hey, I watered and fed the horses. Least you can do is feed us."

The temptation to offer to water him, too, by throwing him back into the creek, was great, but Gerard resisted. "If I cook, you have to eat what I cook. Sure you're ready for that?" Ailis and Newt had handled the limited cooking detail the last time they were on the road, and for a good reason: Gerard's rabbits always came out half-raw, and the birds half-burned. He could mend armor, wield a sword, brandish a mace reasonably well, and ride a horse better than most, but he couldn't cook.

They started walking back to the camp together, pausing to set up a picket line for the horses. A rope tied between two stakes in the ground would allow the horses to move around and graze at will, but would keep them from wandering off in the night. The mule didn't need tethering—it was smarter than the horses, and would be fine no matter what.

"You think she's all right?" There was no need for Newt to say whom he was talking about: No matter what other mission Merlin might have for them, no matter what the king might think, Ailis was the whole reason they were there.

"I don't think Morgain's hurt her, if that's what you mean," Gerard said slowly, finally allowing himself to speak it out loud. It was easier to worry about Sir Caedor than to imagine Ailis alone and frightened. "Merlin was right about that. Whatever reason the sorceress had for taking her, she did have a reason. And I don't think it was just to keep Ailis from telling anyone that Morgain was in Camelot. Otherwise, why not kill her right there in some way that wouldn't raise questions?"

"Maybe she was in a hurry and needed time to do it properly?" Newt caught the look Gerard gave him, and shrugged. "It's possible. I don't want to think about it either, but . . ."

"Merlin would have known if Ailis were . . . hurt." He couldn't bring himself to say dead.

"Maybe." Newt didn't sound convinced. Gerard

113

didn't feel convinced, either. But they had to believe that Ailis was all right.

Morgain hated her half-brother Arthur. And for some reason she hated Merlin even more. But she had shown no sign of hating the three of them, even when they had stopped her from destroying the Grail Quest. Even when Ailis was urging Gerard to kill Morgain, the sorceress had seemed more amused and—perhaps—intrigued by the servant-girl who showed such affinity for magic.

That was the hope Gerard clung to, even as it terrified him. Because he knew—even if Ailis herself didn't—how much appeal magic held for his friend. And from their brief encounter, he knew how appealing Morgain herself could be, if she decided to charm rather than oppose.

"You, boy!" Sir Caedor stood by the fire and pointed to Newt. "Gather some firewood!"

Newt made a sour face and whispered to Gerard, "If I were to pour water over his armor, might it rust shut with him inside it?"

"He'd expect me to polish it all clean again," Gerard said in disgust. There would be time enough to go back to polishing and repairing and running errands when he was back in Camelot with Ailis safely back in the queen's solar.

"Come on," he said with a sigh. "Let's go find some deadwood and give Sir Caedor a nice big comfortable fire to sleep by. Maybe, if we're lucky, he'll tell us some more stories about his great role in the battle of Traeth Tryfrwyd."

Newt stifled a groan and followed Gerard into the underbrush.

TEN

"**B**last it, Merlin! I need more information! How can I rule this island, filled with madmen and magic, without knowing who is doing what, planning what, when, and to whom?"

"You would have a dozen such as myself, could I arrange it, but there is only one Merlin to fly to your lure, my king," Merlin said, settling himself in a chair and sighing like the tired ancient he was.

Arthur looked up at his enchanter. "I need only one. But he needs to stop griping and do what he does best: reassure his liege that the battles are indeed engaged." Arthur was seated on a bench in Merlin's workroom, the same seat Newt had taken not a handful of days before, tapping his fingers on his knee impatiently.

"Gripe, gripe, gripe. I am not the one intruding

on another's space and making impossible demands, Arthur the King." But his mockery was equally affectionate, and the enchanter obligingly closed his eyes and spiraled down into his *sense* of Morgain, the familiar sharp tingle of her personality, the salty flavor of her magic.

* * *

Like the bird he was named for, wings spread and dipping into the wind, following the familiar sense. Eyes were blind, but the sense was true, leading him to the source, the enticing magical aroma that was the sorceress.

And there his wings slammed up against a black wall, invisible until you made contact, and then felt in every point of his non-existent body.

Ow!

She was good. He would admit that freely. She was very very good. He changed form, feathered wings becoming leathery, talons turning into claws that could cling to the walls. He swung upside down and cocked his head—the better not to listen, but to sense.

Morgain, yes. And fainter, far fainter, a tinge of something carrying Merlin's own mark, intentionally placed there for just such a need. Ailis. Alive.

He was about to launch himself off the wall and

return to the safety of his own quarters when something else moved. Faintly, faintly, barely sounding behind Morgain's protections, but . . . there. Something new. Something unsettling. Something foreign.

A whiplash of unknown power slapped the bat off the wall and sent it tumbling back into the ether, tumbling claws over head, even as Merlin struggled to regain control.

He thought, as he changed form back to the more familiar bird of prey; something did not want him there, not anywhere near Morgain or her distant tower, or whatever she might be plotting there. . . .

* * *

"Are you all right, my Merlin?" Arthur asked.

The enchanter coughed, his chest painful inside and out, as though he had been kicked by an irate plow-horse, and he waved his king away. "I'm fine," he said quietly, his eyes turned inward. "I'm fine."

Forgive me, children, Merlin thought. *Forgive me for sending you into danger I had not foreseen. Forgive me for waking something that should have remained unaware.*

Forgive me for not being able to help you, now.

* * *

"And there I was, standing tall despite my horse having been taken down moments before. Arthur fought on beside me, magnificent as ever, but it was my responsibility to defend his left flank, and not allow any barbarian to reach him with sword or spear. . . ."

Newt had fallen asleep some time earlier, but he was propped up against an old log so it looked as though he were still listening intently. Gerard actually *was* listening, although exhaustion was starting to overtake him as well.

The story was interesting, especially considering that his own master, Sir Rheynold, had never been all that fond of "danger and adventure at all costs," despite riding willingly into battle at Arthur's command. But after living with and around knights and more ordinary fighters for almost half his life, Gerard knew how battlefield exploits could and would become exaggerated. And the more time that passed between battle and retelling, the more exaggerated the stories would become.

The battle Sir Caedor was telling them about had taken place before either boy was born. By those standards, the entire story might be myth. But even if so, it was an entertaining myth. Gerard finally fell asleep, and dreamt of epic battles of his own.

*　*　*

Gerard woke to find the sun barely peeking over the hills, but Sir Caedor was already awake, practicing in a clearing a few feet away from the fire. He had put aside his armor, and, clad only in his pants and a sleeveless jerkin, had drawn a beautiful sword tempered to a dull gloss, and a smaller but no less deadly looking long dagger. He thrust and parried with the dagger in his right hand, even as the left arm drew back the sword, raising it to make a killing blow while his phantom opponents were distracted by the dagger. He pivoted seamlessly on his back leg, his forefoot carrying him into the attack of a phantom behind him. His dagger swung high, to threaten the eyes of a new opponent. It was all graceful and unhurried, his movements perfectly balanced, from the loose set of his shoulders to the way he rocked back and forward on his feet as he moved.

"He's good, isn't he?" Newt asked. He was awake, lying on his side and wrapped in his blanket with his backside to the coals of the fire, watching the knight thrust and parry.

"Yes. Yes, he is," Gerard said, sitting up to better observe. He had never realized quite how good.

Although there was a world of difference between practicing weapon forms in a peaceful clearing and fighting in the thick of battle, Sir Caedor had done both.

Sir Caedor was very, very good. And Gerard suddenly understood a little better why the king and Merlin had chosen the seasoned soldier to go with them. Not because they had thought that the two boys might need protection—or because they didn't think the boys could carry out both parts of their mission—but because they could learn from seeing this experience in action. *Ignore the stories,* he could almost hear Arthur say. *Ignore the snobbery. Look to the man.*

It didn't make the knight's attitude any less annoying. But it gave Gerard a reason to look past it, to see the dedication, the power in his arms and shoulders, the focus given to his art.

He didn't know how to say any of that to Newt. The stable boy would never be allowed to fight with sword and shield, never ride any of the horses he cared for into battle. He would never stand shoulder to shoulder with his brother knights to protect the innocent and defend the kingdom. It wasn't fair, but Newt's birth would forever keep him from the ranks of knights and landowners. So what use was Sir Caedor's knowledge—and what protection did he have against Caedor's cutting remarks?

Gerard lay back down on the ground with a sigh, crossing the back of one arm over his eyes as though to block out the awareness of another day ahead of them.

All he wanted to do was free Ailis and go home.

ELEVEN

Ailis had spent the night twisting and turning in the comfortable bed in her comfortable bed-chamber, staring out the window at the gray sky washing into the gray sea. She plotted ways to escape until she fell asleep to dream of riding Sir Tawny through impossible underwater canyons made of whitewashed stone.

Waking brought the realization that she was no closer to finding a way out of the fortress. The air was only beginning to lighten, the sun rising on the other side of the compound, when Morgain herself arrived at the door of Ailis's chamber. The girl had been sitting at the window, looking at the dark waves while brushing out her hair, when the sorceress walked in without bothering to knock. The usual magically propelled breakfast cart waited behind her, bearing twice as much food as days past.

The sorceress looked vastly different from the last time Ailis had seen the woman face to face. In her throne room on the Isle of Apples, Morgain had been dressed in a lovely gown, bejeweled and almost blindingly beautiful. Now, although her beauty remained, she wore a more demure outfit. Her hair was pulled away from her face with narrow braids, one tucked behind each ear, and she had simple slippers like those Ailis wore.

The sorceress said nothing, merely allowing the cart to roll itself in. Then she helped herself to a share of the food. Taking her cue from that, Ailis put aside her need to assault the woman with questions, and settled in to satisfy her own hunger.

When the last flaky pastry and slab of sausage had been consumed, Morgain washed her fingers in the bowl of water set aside for that purpose, and held out her clean hand for Ailis to take.

"Come with me, witch-child."

Ailis resisted expressing her initial reaction to the nickname, and allowed herself to be escorted into the hallway. There was nothing to be gained by annoying her captor, apart from being turned into a fish, or something more cruel.

The sorceress brought her down a staircase one level, leading the girl to a room filled floor to ceiling with books and parchments and maps. Most of them were in languages Ailis could not recognize, much less understand, but she was fascinated. Who knew there were so many sheets of paper on the entire island? Morgain walked from shelf to shelf, taking down one book then another, putting together a pile that she said "might be of interest, and a way to pass the time."

"I don't want to pass the time." If Ailis had stopped to think, she would never have dared speak back to the sorceress, but the words simply came out of her mouth. "I want to go home."

"I know, witch-child, I know," Morgain said. Her tone was disturbingly gentle, the way adults sound when they're about to tell you something really, really bad. "You can't go home. Not just yet. But I will not allow you to waste away, witch-child, no fears."

What could Ailis say? She had no weapons to fight her way free, no way to contact Merlin to rescue her, no way to do anything but submit. She made a dutiful curtsey, shallower than she might have to the queen, which merely made Morgain laugh. Ailis took the parchments and books back to her room, and piled them on a small table that appeared next to the sofa. A gorgeous quilt, with gold and blue and green and deep purple squares, was draped across the back of the sofa, its texture softer and warmer than anything she had ever felt before.

"If you have need of anything else," Morgain said, "just ask." She stood in the doorway watching Ailis with a strange sort of satisfaction on her face, almost as though she didn't know how to express what she was feeling, or even how to feel it at all.

"Ask who?" The thought of someone listening in on her at all times made Ailis suddenly feel self-conscious. She looked around nervously, as though something would suddenly be revealed.

"Ah, yes." It was clear that Morgain had never thought of such a discomfort, and Ailis suspected that she was so accustomed to having servants underfoot that she never saw them. Though to be fair, Ailis had not seen any servants at all since that first morning. Were they discreet? Absent for some sort of holiday? Or had Morgain turned them all invisible for some reason? Might they be lurking anywhere, everywhere, watching all the time?

"Here," and the sorceress stepped forward into the room, casting her gaze around until she saw what she was looking for. "Here." She picked up a small silver candlestick and touched it with her free hand. A blue-green spark jumped from her fingertip to the top of the candlestick, and a slender foam-colored candle appeared in the previously empty socket.

The sorceress considered the result, then nodded with satisfaction. "Light this when you wish to make a request. Someone will hear you. Is that acceptable?"

"Yes. Thank you." Ailis looked away, trying desperately to remind herself that despite the kindness and consideration this woman was showing her, she was still an evil sorceress, a wicked woman who had tried to destroy Camelot, had threatened her and her friends, had stolen her away from her home, and was keeping her a prisoner.

Any more a prisoner than you were in the queen's solar? Any more a prisoner than you were, tied to the roles they want you in, not the one you *want?*

To that small voice inside her own head, Ailis was unable to respond. And when she looked up again, Morgain was gone.

* * *

The next afternoon, Morgain again appeared for a brief time, interrupting a nap filled with disturbingly vivid dreams. This time the enchantress took Ailis to the far tower, where they stood by a huge open window and watched seabirds circle and dive into the ocean.

"I've never seen birds so large."

"There are none larger on this isle, and indeed, few larger anywhere," Morgain said. "They are warriors, in their own right."

"I've dreamt . . ." Ailis stopped, suddenly shy, then plowed forward again. "I've dreamt of flying like that."

"Have you now?" Morgain asked, her head cocked in curiosity. Then the sorceress raised her left hand, and made a movement with four of her five fingers. A strange noise rose from her slender throat as she did so. One of the birds, not quite as massive as the others, broke away from his circling and came closer—close enough that a sleek white feather fell from its wing, spiraling down in a lazy eddy, directly into Morgain's upraised fingers.

Almost as long as Ailis's hand, the feather gleamed with sea spray and some strange iridescent sparkle that seemed to come from within the quill itself.

"A talisman of your own," Morgain said, a sly

reference to the last time they had met.

Ailis tucked the feather into the knot of her braid, where she could feel it occasionally brushing against her back. Then they descended the tower into a huge dining hall, where the afternoon meal was laid out: the most incredible food Ailis had ever tasted, beginning with a soup made from fresh berries, followed by a massive baked fish, crisp tubers, crusted bread that steamed when she broke it open to discover butter already melted inside, and a strange vegetable that looked too spiny to be edible but tasted wonderful.

Faintly visible ghostly servants moved platters around and refilled empty glasses, then retreated against the wall to wait until they were needed again. Ailis wondered if they were real people, ghosts, or, perhaps, purely magical constructs. Did they serve willingly? Did magical creatures care who they served? Was this to be her fate, someday? And could she possibly convince any of them to help her?

Raising a hand, she indicated to one that she would like more wine. Watching carefully, Ailis saw a figure look to Morgain first for permission. So much for that. If it needed approval to even give more refreshment, helping Ailis to leave without Morgain's knowledge was out of the question.

"Do you like the sturgeon?"

"It's quite good."

And it was, along with everything else at the meal. They sat at a long table, covered with a cloth of shimmering white linen and set with plates of polished metal that glowed in the candlelight, goblets of crystal filled with dark ruby wine, and horn-handled eating instruments that might be useful as weapons, were she to slip them into her pocket and take them away from the table.

And now, as the translucent servants cleared away the meal's dishes, another platter floated in, this one was covered in bite-sized pastries, cunningly made in the shapes of miniature animals. Ailis, after looking to Morgain for permission and receiving an encouraging nod, chose a white stag. Biting into it revealed a fruited filling that filled Ailis's mouth with a tart, tangy sensation.

"Pears," Morgain said, in response to Ailis's happy sigh. "There's nothing quite like a pear."

Awash in a strange contentment that seemed to come from nowhere, Ailis was willing to take her word for it. The thought that this was magic, all magic, and she might well be under an enchantment, flitted through the girl's mind. But since she couldn't do anything about it if it were so, Ailis let the notion pass, and chose another pastry: a unicorn with an impossibly tiny gilded horn.

The unicorn was halfway to her mouth when the doors behind her crashed open. Ailis froze, an instinctive response. Morgain's face seemed to tell her to stay still and say nothing.

"Woman, you have lied to me!"

Morgain smoothed the fabric of her dress and rose to meet the newcomer, one of her well-groomed eyebrows raised in a calculated expression of surprise. "Be careful what you say, my friend. Bursting into my presence with such an accusation might be considered ill-manners. What is this lie you claim that I have told?"

"That!" From the way Morgain's gaze did not shift, the girl suspected that she was the subject of the spiteful voice's words. But she remained very still, very silent, wishing for the ability to turn translucent like the sorceress's servants. "The agreement was that none were to know I was here."

"And no one does. And no one would have, had you not burst in here like an ill-mannered child."

Don't look, child, a voice in Ailis's head warned her. *Don't turn, don't move, don't look. . . .*

Merlin? But while familiar, the voice did not feel like the enchanter's, not entirely. *Morgain?* No response.

"You did not tell me you had brought this one here. Why?"

"Because I did not trust you to behave," Morgain said. Her back was straight and her voice was steady, though a careful observer might have detected a faint tremor in her hand.

"She is—"

"She is a guest in my house," Morgain said. "As are you."

There was tension in this room that terrified Ailis more than she had ever been before; even more than when she hid under the low bed in her parents' cottage and heard the sounds of battle raging all around her; even more than coming out of that cottage and seeing bodies strewn about her village. This wasn't violence or madness. Those memories were hot and fierce. This was cold and severe; it whispered around her soul like the sound of a frigid winter's wind.

There was a long silence, before the door was slammed shut again. Morgain held herself very still, but for the rise and fall of her chest as she took a long breath in, then let it out in an equally long and slow movement.

"I am afraid I need to ask you to stay in your rooms . . . until I can decide what to do with you," she said, not looking at Ailis. "I will have someone continue to bring meals, and whatever books or amusements you desire. It is . . . temporary, I promise."

Temporary because she would go home soon? Temporary because she would be allowed to roam the castle again? Or temporary because . . . Ailis decided not to finish that thought. All she knew was that she didn't want to be anywhere near that shadowy voice. She wanted it to forget she ever existed, and never see her ever again.

Morgain scared her and made her angry—but she had to admit Morgain also fascinated her. But the speaker of that voice terrified her. The fact that she didn't know *why* she was so terrified only made it worse. But she would not give the sorceress the satisfaction of knowing that. *Strength,* she thought. *She respects strength as well as talent, especially in females.*

"I think I would very much like to return to my room now," she said, standing up on legs that were only a little shaky. "With your permission . . ."

Morgain merely nodded, her mind clearly

leagues away on some other matter. "I shall escort you." Not because Ailis did not know the way, and not, the girl suspected, because Morgain feared Ailis might try to escape. The only other reason was that the intruder might be lurking, waiting for her somewhere in the hallways between here and there, and neither female believed that the results of such a meeting would be pleasant for Ailis.

And for the first time, the restrictions that had kept her trapped before, now seemed comforting.

*　*　*

The three rescuers had been riding since dawn that day, following the tug of the lodestone that hung around Gerard's neck. Both Gerard and Newt had been awake before the sun, lying in their bedrolls, silently wrapped in their own bleak thoughts, until Sir Caedor woke and went through his now-expected morning routine. That was Newt's cue to build the fire back up and start breakfast, while Gerard fed and watered the horses. It might have made more sense to do it the other way around, but Sir Caedor's manner set off a stubborn reaction in both boys. They had gone about the other's normal chores with a studied cheerfulness.

That had been many hours ago. Gerard felt as though his backside had somehow merged with his saddle sometime between the noon meal and now. The daily routine back home of weapons-practice and classes and more practice seemed so much easier than merely sitting on horseback.

"You're sure there's an inn ahead?" Gerard asked.

"I am certain," Sir Caedor replied, leaning back to take the waterskin Gerard was passing him as they rode. "Your uncle and I stayed there while paying a visit on the warleader, ah, what was his name . . . Ragnar? A heathen Norseman who thought to set himself up as competition."

That was a story Gerard had heard before, how his uncle Kay had met the Norse warrior and bested him thrice: once on the battlefield, once at the banquet table, and once in a contest of song. Never before had he heard that Sir Caedor had traveled on the same quest, but then Kay was not the most modest of men, and he would not have willingly shared his story with another.

The sun had fallen below the tree line some time ago. The light around them had darkened in response, but since the lodestone seemed to point in the direction of the supposed inn, Gerard had given the go-ahead to continue on. If it would sweeten Sir Caedor's mood for the evening, the next day might go more smoothly.

The only drawback was that the horses were more likely to stumble when they could not see the road. The air was filled with the dusk chorus of birds and insects, intercut every now and again by the cry of a distant wolf. Gerard had looked at Newt when the first howl sounded, but when the other boy seemed unconcerned, the squire decided it wasn't something he should be worrying about, either. Even more telling, while his horse had started at the first note, the mule still trotted along placidly.

Gerard just wished that they would arrive at the inn already, to put an end to this conversation, if nothing else. Being caught between the two, friend and knight, was making him feel horribly uncomfortable, and caused his wound to itch horribly. He noticed that Newt was having the same trouble, often interrupting his words to scratch irritably at his own scab.

Sir Caedor finished drinking from the waterskin, wiped his mouth with the back of his arm, and handed the skin to Newt, diving right back into an ongoing debate. "Your faith does you credit, boy. But yes, my experience tells me otherwise. It's been almost a week since the girl was taken. Deep down inside, you know that she's most likely dead by now. Or worse."

Newt glared at the knight. "There's nothing worse than being dead."

Sir Caedor made a sound low in his throat, filled with pity at Newt's innocence. But Gerard knew what his friend meant. You never got another chance after death. Anything else . . . anything else, you could come back from.

That was Ailis. Solid, strong, dependable. She could come back from anything.

"Well, if she's dead, why are we still going after her?" Newt's voice was stern, almost bitter in his challenge, and Gerard tensed.

Sir Caedor surprised him, though. "To avenge her, if needed. To bring her body home. To care for her, as is our sworn duty, as knights—and as men of our word." This was the kindest thing Caedor had said about Newt until now, even indirectly. "To bring that sorceress to justice, once and for all."

Gerard almost fell off his horse at that last bit. The three of them? Take down Morgain against her will? Sir Caedor must have gotten into the berries they always warned the pages about, because he sounded like he was hallucinating. Not even Merlin could do anything about Morgain—or rather, he could, but would not because Arthur would not allow it. She was evil and treacherous and dangerous . . . and she was the daughter of Arthur's mother, the girl who had once held the baby Arthur in her arms. A fact that the king never, ever forgot, and woe to the man who thought it wasn't important.

Newt slumped deeper into his saddle, almost becoming one with the leather and wood, and refused to look at the knight. He stared straight between Loyal's ears at the road in front of them.

Sir Caedor, having gotten no response, kicked his horse into a slightly faster trot and rode on ahead.

"I do worry . . ." Gerard said.

"About what?" Newt asked.

"Ailis. Being with Morgain all that time. Being around magic, and not good magic."

Newt tightened his grip on his reins again, then relaxed Loyal back into a slow, steady walk. "There is no good magic. She shouldn't be around any of it at all."

"Not even Merlin's?" Gerard knew he was poking a sleeping boar with a short spear, but he couldn't stop. "The kind of magic that we've been using to save our very precious skins? The magic that animates the lodestone? The magic that keeps fires from destroying villages and clears muck from wells? Are we going to go through *that* argument again?"

Newt shrugged, looking away as though wanting to pretend they weren't having this conversation. But the topic of magic had been simmering—and boiling over—too many times since Gerard had met the other boy, and there never seemed to be a reason for it. Time to confront the question head-on. Newt's unease around magic might become a real problem down the road. It might help to know *why* he reacted that way, just in case.

So Gerard took a deep breath, and plunged in. "Why are you so opposed to magic, anyway? I mean, I know that Sir Gawain thinks it's an affront against God, but that doesn't seem to be your thing. . . ."

"It's . . . a long story."

"We've got nothing but time right now. Unless you'd rather Sir Caedor talk to us some more about his long and glorious career. . . ."

Newt gave a dramatic shudder, settling himself even deeper in the saddle and reaching up to rub again at his face. As Gerard had suspected, the words that came out of his mouth after touching the scar were gentler, more even-tempered. "Anything but that! I'm not sure I could deal with yet another retelling of the Battle of Deeply Impressive Me, as told through his much more *experienced* point of view."

Gerard checked to make sure that Sir Caedor hadn't been close enough to overhear.

"Tell me again, why did Merlin think we needed an adult along?" Newt asked, clearly trying to change the subject away from himself and magic. "And why this particular adult? You think maybe it was because Arthur didn't want him hanging around Camelot?"

Gerard almost choked. "Okay, that was cruel. Possibly true, but cruel." But he wasn't going to let Newt slip away that easily. "Magic, Newt. You're using it now, don't you feel it? The warmth from the scar? That's Merlin's spell working in you."

"Yeah. Thought it might be." Newt didn't seem particularly excited by the idea.

"And it's keeping you from doing—or saying— anything you know is really stupid?"

"Mostly."

"So what's the problem?"

"There is no problem."

Gerard let that one pass for a bit without saying anything, then he asked again, "What's the problem?"

"Ger . . ."

"Newt . . . come on. Why can't you ever admit to anything? Newt's not even your real name, is it?"

"No." Newt was clearly reluctant to admit even that, although it wasn't exactly a secret. As a nickname it was bad enough. To be named that by your parents—that was hard to imagine.

"So . . . ?"

"So, it's not my real name. I've been called that since I was barely crawling. I don't even remember my real name anymore." Newt's voice was wistful. Then, as though realizing he had given something away, he hardened his voice back to the brash, rough-and-tumble stable boy Gerard had first met. "Not that it matters what anyone yells, so long as they leave me to get my work done."

"And magic—"

"Has no part in my work. Let it alone, Gerard. Let it alone."

Gerard gave up for now. They both knew that the subject would not be forgotten. When Ailis was safe. When Morgain was no longer a threat.

With an inward laugh, Gerard admitted that he had been beaten. Newt would always be able to find some crisis he could claim was more important than his past. That just made Gerard all the more curious.

He *would* find out, eventually. . . .

TWELVE

"You have been very patient," Morgain said. Ailis jumped in shock. She had been sitting on the divan in front of the fireplace, paging through one of the books the sorceress had given her. Ailis could not read any of the writing. It was in some strange, flowing script that she had never seen before, but the drawings of fantastical beasts and monsters were so beautifully rendered that she almost didn't need the words.

She missed Sir Tawny. The griffin could not fit into her room, and in the several days since that frightening episode at her meal with Morgain, she no longer felt comfortable wandering the hallways with him, not knowing if that whispering shadow-figure was still within the same walls, *watching her*.

"I haven't had much choice, except to be patient,"

Ailis said in response, once her heart settled back into a normal rhythm.

Morgain had simply walked into the sitting room without so much as a knock on the door. Ailis supposed that, as a prisoner, she shouldn't expect any such courtesy. The bitterness behind that thought surprised her; she had never thought herself a grudge-holder. Then again, she hadn't thought herself the type to talk back to a sorceress, or pet a griffin, or dream of blasting open doors with just a twitch of her hand, either.

"True," Morgain acknowledged Ailis's words. She sat down on the sofa next to her and smoothed the fabric of her skirt. The outfit today was a serviceable royal blue woolen, but she had boots on, indicating that she had been outside. "But you have borne it with . . . surprising dignity, for one your age."

Ailis waited. Four days of eating alone, without even ghostly servants for company, had left her feeling adrift, alone in a way she had never known before. Her entire life, from the very first moment she could remember, she had been surrounded by people on all sides. While she hoped that Morgain's reappearance meant that the mysterious stranger had left the castle and she would again be free to roam, she knew that the sorceress's sudden reappearance might mean another kind of end to her captivity. Ailis had no desire whatsoever to die.

No matter what happened, at least she wasn't alone anymore. Even the chatter of the ladies in the solar was better than being alone all the time. She had tried reaching out to Merlin with her thoughts, but to no avail. Either she didn't have the ability, despite what he had said (likely), or he wasn't listening (also likely). Or, most probably, Morgain had protected her stronghold against magics other than her own.

She was totally dependent upon Morgain now, for everything, even companionship.

"Would . . ."

Something about the sorceress's voice distracted Ailis from her own self-pity. Morgain seemed almost awkward. And angry about feeling awkward, Ailis decided.

"Would you care to see my workspace?" Morgain finished.

All of Ailis's thoughts of bitterness disappeared with that offer. She almost fell on her face, leaping up from the divan without untangling herself from the blanket around her lap.

"I . . . yes, I would," she said, trying to regain what little dignity might be left after that. She wasn't going to die! At least, not right now. Not without seeing more of the fortress.

Morgain, although clearly amused, merely indicated with a tilt of her hand that Ailis should put on her slippers and follow her.

This time they used a staircase Ailis had not encountered before. It was a short, very steep staircase that seemed to lead nowhere for a surprisingly long time before depositing them in front of a thick blackwood door without any handle or grate.

"Let me in," Morgain said in a voice that brooked no argument, and made a slight gesture with her left hand. The door opened; not outward, but slid sideways into the wall itself. The sorceress didn't seem to take note of anything wondrous there, but entered, carrying Ailis along by the sheer force of her casualness.

The room sang to her. The tidiness of it all was so different from Merlin's disaster of a study. This room appealed to Ailis's organized nature, and the flavor of magic that she had become so attuned to in the rest of the fortress, almost without realizing it, practically pooled in the air around her here.

There was an oaken table in the center, hip-high, so that Morgain might work at it standing or seated on one of the stools pulled up to its side. The surface was battered and scarred from years of heavy use, but the quality of the table still shone through. Its inner sheen reminded Ailis of tales of the Round Table, although otherwise the two had nothing whatsoever in common.

Drawing her gaze away from the table, Ailis looked around the rest of the room. Like so much in the keep, the room was larger than it seemed it should be from the outside. Shelves lined the walls, and there were racks and cabinets holding strange objects, some of which seemed to shimmer when you looked at them indirectly. There was a cozy sort of clutter to it all, and it felt more like a blacksmith's workshop than a magician's study.

Whatever it reminded her of, it fascinated her. The memory of all the things she knew about Morgain's magic being bad and unnatural and purely wrong faded. Ailis let herself be seated on a small wooden stool next to Morgain, who started lifting powders and vials from a rack on the wall and placing them in a very definite order on the battered surface of the wooden table.

Ailis watched in silence for a few moments as a purple liquid was mixed with a powder of tiny golden flecks. The result was poured into a glass vial closed with a wax stopper, then shaken firmly and turned upside down to rest. Morgain studied the vial carefully, so Ailis did as well. Then curiosity overcame her.

"What are we looking for?"

"The goldstone extract should react to the enathras to form a solid," Morgain said, gesturing at the purple liquid, distilled from flowers that grew on a vine on the outside walls.

"Out of liquid?"

Morgain gave Ailis a look. "Have you never made stew?"

Ailis had, of course, but the thought of Morgain the Sorceress, user of Old Magics, mistress of this fortress, in this very room making something as homely as stew, was hard to imagine.

"So the flecks act like heat, to draw the liquid away?"

"Very good. Not quite accurate, but it shows a basic grasp. The characteristics of goldstone are that of extraction and transformation. An alchemist would no doubt spin you some complicated theory on how it all works.

"Alchemy, you should know, is the province of fools and madmen who think to cheat the Universe. Magic—proper magic—knows that we are all part of the Universe, and must dance to her tune. And if we dance well enough, and please her with our skill, she returns gifts in equal measure."

Morgain returned her attention to the vial, then gave a pleased little exclamation. "Ah, there it is!"

Ailis squinted, and in the middle of the murky purple liquid, she thought that she could see a slightly more solid shape.

"What is it used for?" She wasn't sure what she would be told: a poison, perhaps? Or a curse—something to choke a rival, or blight a crop?

"It is to ease stiffness in the fingers, from the sea-cold," Morgain said instead.

Ailis must have let her astonishment show, because the sorceress laughed. "The folk who live off the ocean are a hardy sort, but even they suffer from her moods. We barter, they and I: A share of their catch feeds me and mine, and a small portion of my work sustains them."

"So it's an ointment?" That was all Ailis had ever heard of that helped such pains, a messy salve that smelled bad enough to empty the area around the stillroom for the rest of the day after they bottled it.

"No, a charm. You wear it around your wrist on a string of ox hide, like a trinket, and it sends ease into the bones. It's a little thing, hardly worth my energy or talents. But it is what they need, and are willing to trade for."

Underneath Morgain's dismissal of this "trinket," Ailis could hear a subtle pride. Not the sort that the sorceress had shown in their earlier meetings, but the kind Newt showed occasionally, when he talked about the horses he helped to train. Or of work done, and done well, no matter how seemingly small in the scheme of things.

A well-trained horse would not become skittish in battle and throw his rider. A healthy fisherman would not allow his family to starve, come the winter storms.

And work well-done is the mark of a craftsman—or woman—worth the hire.

This did not sit well with the accepted view of Morgain, the view Morgain herself provoked and maintained, of the vengeful and dangerous sorceress. Of the *evil* woman, set on taking down her brother's rightful claim to the title of High King.

It puzzled Ailis. So she did what she did with all

things that puzzled her. She put it away in a corner of her mind, and went on with what was in front of her.

"What is this?" she asked, pointing to a series of linked crystals on the table, glimmering blue and gold and black deep within the links.

"Those are not for touching. Or looking too deeply in," Morgain said brusquely, reaching up to cover them with a dark cloth, shielding them from Ailis's gaze. "Not everything in this room is so gentle as the bone-warmers."

Ailis knew she should have felt rebuked. Instead, she turned to another object, this one a polished bone the size and shape of a pigeon's wing, set in a block of onyx. "And this?"

Morgain looked, then smiled. "That, my dear, is for a woman whose man strays."

"It brings him back home?"

"In a manner of speaking, yes." Morgain's smile twitched, but she refused to elaborate further.

All right, perhaps that might be something evil. Or not. Ailis wasn't sure—and she wasn't sure she wanted to know.

"Here, try this." Morgain lifted a flat piece of wood off the table and handed it to Ailis. The girl took it hesitantly, almost expecting it to transform into something dangerous, or at least surprising. But it remained a piece of wood.

"Tell me about it," Morgain demanded.

Ailis looked at Morgain, then back at the wood.

"It's wood." She ran one finger along the length of the piece. "A soft wood, not hard. Birch?" Morgain didn't respond, instead turning to a box of tiny metal figures which she began to sort, almost as though they were threads for embroidery.

The thought made Ailis nostalgic for an instant, for the boring sameness of the queen's solar. Then she looked down at the wood in her hands, and was absorbed again in the task set to her.

"It has been planed, smoothed. So it's not meant for whittling. Birch isn't used for building, nor tools. My cousin . . ." Ailis stopped. She hadn't thought of her cousin in years. He was dead now, in the same battle that took her parents, and his parents as well. He would have been a man now, had he lived. "My cousin used to make boats out of birch bark." Ailis stroked the wood some more, lost in her memories.

Birch is the wood of memory. The wood of remembrance.

The voice didn't sound like Merlin's. It didn't

sound like Morgain's, either. Deeper, more rounded, more feminine than either, and yet powerful at the same time, and it came not from outside Ailis's mind, but somewhere deeper inside. It was the same voice that had warned her away from looking at the figure behind her in the dining hall.

"It's meant to . . . hold things? A box, or a chest . . . no." Visions came to her then, of the shelves in Merlin's study, the upper reaches of Morgain's library. "Spellbooks. It's used to bind spellbooks."

"To bind, yes, and it's often used as the pages themselves," Morgain said. "For things that are best carved, not written with anything as flimsy as ink."

Ailis looked at the blank wood and tried to visualize what sort of spells might be best carved rather than penned. She could almost see the heated prong etching runes into the pale wood, red and char marking the smooth surface in a mockery of the magical characters Merlin had drawn with fire on ice when he gave them the riddle to find the talisman to break Morgain's sleep-spell.

"You mean a dangerous spell. One that hurts people," Ailis said.

"Spells are just words, witch-child. They don't do anything, of themselves. A spell to drive the

153

strength from a man's body is only a word removed from the one that drives infection from a wound. I've cast both, in my time. And will cast them both again. It all depends upon who is asking, and why."

"And how much you hate them." Ailis said, daring greatly, speaking for the first time of the one thing that everyone knew. "The way you hate the king."

Morgain's hands stilled at her task.

"Yes," she said quietly. "How very much I hate."

THIRTEEN

The air smelled of warm horseflesh and dry straw, with an undertone of mold and rot. It was familiar and comforting and disgusting, all at once. Somewhere off to the right side of Gerard's head, a bug was making a soft chirping noise.

"You awake?"

"No." Gerard kept his eyes closed, hoping that Newt would take the hint.

"This is a nice inn."

"Yes, it is."

"Supper was really good."

"Yes, it was." Gerard wished that Newt would get to the point already and let him sleep.

"We should remember to tell Sir Caedor that in the morning—that it's a good inn, I mean. Since he chose it."

Gerard rolled over on his side and stared at Newt across the stall they were sleeping in. The hay crinkled underneath, bits of it poking through the blanket and scratching his skin—a small price to pay for the smell and sounds of the horses kept in the stalls on either side of them. But the hay was clean and dry, and there was a roof overhead.

"Out of the only two we saw all day, yes. We should tell him. Newt, what are you up to?"

"Me?"

"Yes, you." He was beginning to remember why his first act upon meeting Newt had been to blacken the other boy's eye.

Newt flopped onto his back, exhaling heavily. "Nothing. Really. I just thought it would soften him up a little."

"And?" Gerard didn't know if it was Arthur's wisdom or Merlin's cunning, or just his own knowledge of the fact that Newt didn't care a whit about Sir Caedor, but he could tell there was a logic at work that had nothing to do with the knight's mood, softened or otherwise.

"And if things were better between the two of us, you could sleep in the inn itself, the way you should. And not spend the night in a stable like—"

"Like a stable boy?"

"Yes."

"Newt . . ." Gerard tried to figure out how to get his point across without using the wrong words or making things worse somehow. "If I had wanted to sleep in the inn, I would have. But they only had one room, even with our script from the king authorizing whatever we needed, and only one bed in that room. I would rather sleep in the stable. *Without* straw."

Gerard lay back down and stared at the wooden ceiling. "Besides. He snores."

"Fair enough. So do you."

"I do not!"

"Sure you don't," Newt said soothingly.

Gerard snorted and pulled his blanket up over his shoulder, indicating that the conversation was at an end, and he was, by God, going to sleep.

"I heard what you said," Newt said softly, almost to himself. "To Sir Caedor, before supper. Thank you."

There really wasn't anything to say to that. So Gerard was silent.

*   *   *

In the small but comfortable room in the Oak Tree Inn, Sir Caedor lay on a narrow bed and stared at the whitewashed wood-beam ceiling. He had wanted nothing to do with this journey. He was supposed to be preparing for the Quest to find the Grail—the greatest undertaking in the history of Britain, the crowning achievement of Arthur's reign. Instead, he was playing nursemaid to two boys who clearly saw him as nothing more than a hindrance to their own headstrong ways.

Arthur had warned him of this. "They are young yet, and while tested and proven in courage and skills, their experiences are limited. Be their wise right arm, their protector. Do this, and you shall be rewarded."

In his quieter moments, Caedor could see that it made sense. He was to be young Gerard's protector, his teacher. And the best way to teach was often not to lead, but to allow the student to lead, and correct him when he went wrong.

But Gerard did not take well to being corrected. This afternoon had been a perfect example of that.

*   *   *

"We will have your best rooms. And supper, a full supper. Newt, take the horses to the stable, and ensure that they are taken care of." Sir Caedor swung down from his saddle, bringing out from inside his tunic the script from Arthur—a sheet of parchment that gave them the right

to ask for anything short of military aid or treaty, and that Camelot would stand surety for it.

"We have only one room, but it is yours, sir knight. Supper is served in the common room, but I assure you, it is everything you might desire."

The innkeeper was a slimy ball of a man, stuttering and practically salivating over them. Caedor could only imagine how the man thought to turn their presence to his benefit, perhaps charge the locals a coin each to view the bed the "famed knight from Camelot" slept in, or to eat from the same bowl he used.

"You will stay a night? Two nights? Longer? We can accommodate you better the next night, I will have another room open for your squires."

"Thank you, no. We will have need only for one night." Gerard butted into the conversation before Caedor could inform the innkeeper of the same thing. The man looked taken aback that a squire would interrupt his master, and Caedor could feel his jaw begin to grind in frustration.

"If you have only the one room," Gerard continued, "Newt and I will bed down with the horses. But the meal would be most welcome." The stable boy, who had hung back while Caedor spoke, nodded and led the horses off.

When the innkeeper bowed and scurried off to make

the room ready, Caedor turned to face his charge.

"There was no need to offer to sleep with the horses. I'm certain he could have found a room for you."

"We have discussed this before," the squire said, leaving Caedor at a loss. "You must treat Newt with more respect, or we will leave you here, despite Arthur's request that we include you in our journey."

The squire stared him directly in the eye in a way that could only be described as defiant. "I mean it. I will leave you here, and report back that you failed in your obligation—failed in the basic task of showing courtesy and respect to your companions."

Caedor's jaw worked, but no words came out. How dare this youth, this stripling, this child say such things to him? To reprimand him over how he treated a mere stable boy?

"Accept Newt as a travel companion, not a servant," the squire said. "Or stay here on the morning when we leave."

* * *

Lying in bed, staring at the ceiling, Caedor knew what he would do when the sun rose. Duty was duty. But it left a bitter taste in his mouth; the taste of ashes and saltwater.

*   *   *

Ailis had no idea what time it was. She wasn't even really sure what day it was. One faded into the next, no way to set one day off from another. After a while, it didn't matter. But her brain, confused and filled with new and strange information, could not let go of one question: "Why did you steal me?"

Morgain didn't bother to look up from the parchment she was reading. "Focus on the spell, witch-child."

"I *am* focused." Ailis thought that she could do this in her sleep at this point. "Why did you steal me from Camelot?"

The enchantress gave a dramatic sigh, placing the parchment down carefully on her workbench. "Have you never seen a shiny button on the ground and picked it up?"

Ailis didn't need to have it explained further. Morgain had taken her not from any planned intent, but because she thought that Ailis might possibly be useful in some way, at some later time. Or not.

And if not, she would face the fate of all unmatched buttons: being discarded.

Ailis pursed her lips into a tight line, and focused

again on the small silver globe floating in the air in front of her. She would show the sorceress. She would show Morgain that she was worthy of not being discarded.

As though sensing Ailis's thoughts, Morgain smiled, a sly, smug smile of her own, and rose to walk over to where Ailis was working. She leaned her head of shining dark hair over the girl's red braids to check her progress.

"Gently," she said. "Gently wins the day." Then the two of them leaned forward as one to breathe on the sphere, and it dissolved into a spray of noxious-smelling fumes.

"I did it!" Ailis said jubilantly. "I did it!"

"Yes," Morgain said, leaning back and gazing at her student with pride. "Yes, you did."

In her fascination with the spell's result, Ailis completely missed the dangerous glint of satisfaction in Morgain's eyes.

* * *

"The lodestone says we take the left-hand road." Gerard looked up from the stone hanging from its leather cord over the unfolded parchment. He was getting quite good at reading Merlin's maps. Once you got past the fear of touching a sigil and setting off some unpredictable protective spell, they were remarkably useful things.

"There is nothing there but a small village," Sir Caedor said, dismissing the map and the lodestone. "I do not think a dangerous sorceress would be hiding among the fisherfolk cottages. If she were, even a young girl like your maiden would be able to escape, no? To the right, boys. Follow the road to the right," and he pointed to the fork in the road, to where a small but elaborate watchtower rose. "That is where we must look."

"Does he never tire of being wrong?" Newt asked quietly. He reached up to touch the scab on his face, feeling the warm glow that spread from his hand into his chest when he did so. It had the feel of King Arthur to it, a wry awareness of bigotry and frailty in even the best of men, rather than Merlin's more brusque, abrasive affection. How he knew that, Newt didn't know. But that warmth was all that kept his calm intact, worn to shreds by the endless hard riding and continued uncertainty. Sir Caedor's negative opinion about Ailis's fate was not helping matters, either. The boys were trying so hard to stay optimistic, but every day that passed, and every doom-saying comment by the knight . . .

No. She had to be safe. She *had* to be. Otherwise there was no point to any of it. He didn't care about Morgain, or her plans, or Merlin's power plays. Newt just wanted Ailis to be safe.

"Apparently not," Gerard said in response to Newt's question. The squire folded the map into well-creased quarters and handed it back to his friend. Then he replaced the lodestone around his own neck, where it slipped comfortably under the open collar of his shirt.

"Sir Caedor, the lodestone tells us to take the left-hand path. And so we shall."

The knight muttered under his breath, just as he had every other time Gerard had gainsaid him, but did not protest further.

Finally, Caedor said, "It may be that the village is more important than it looks."

And that, both boys knew, was as much as they would get from Sir Caedor. It was enough.

"Come on," Newt said, swinging back into the saddle and gathering up the reins. Loyal shifted, as impatient as his rider to be done with this traveling. "Every hour we waste is an hour Ailis is waiting."

Left unsaid was the awareness that they might already be too late.

FOURTEEN

"Three touches of air to a dose of water, and . . ." Ailis's memory failed her for a moment. Then the voice she had come to depend upon rose up from inside her and supplied the answer. "Grave dust to fill the air," she finished triumphantly as she meandered through a new hallway.

"So."

A voice came from out of the shadows, before the speaker came into view, scaring all thoughts of spellwork out of her mind completely. Ailis had heard the ladies-in-waiting speak of their blood running cold, but she had dismissed it as foolishness; the overreaction of women who didn't understand fear or fright.

She would have whispered an apology for underestimating them, if she could have found enough moisture in her mouth to form the words.

"So, you are the girl who has interested our hostess, distracted her from that which she must be doing. This costs me time, that I must be here, and not elsewhere."

The speaker stood directly in front of her, but Ailis could not have said what she looked like, or if, in fact, she was indeed female. The voice was a strange whisper, as genderless as the wind, and the body . . .

Ailis could not have focused her gaze on the figure even if she had wanted to. And she didn't. The warning voice in her head was now a scream. *Don't look at the eyes! Don't look! Don't look!* So she only had an impression of a silver-gray robe flowing from cowl to floor; a hooded cloak hiding features in shadows, despite the well-lit hallway they stood in.

The hooded figure leaned in, inspecting Ailis the way a cook might have inspected a chicken brought in from the yard. "What is it about you that is of such import?"

Ailis could only shake her head, unable to even stutter out a disclaimer. She had been working with Morgain most of the morning, helping her set up preparations for a major working. This was the first spellwork Ailis had been allowed to watch. She had felt a strange combination of nerves and excitement which had led to her needing to stretch her legs a bit.

Clearly, leaving the workroom had been a mistake. But if Morgain had known that the shadow-figure had returned, why had she not said anything about it that morning when they began their work? And if the danger from this person had passed . . .

No, the danger certainly had not passed. The danger was right here now. Every instinct she had— ordinary and magical—was screaming at her to turn and run. But there was nowhere *to* run—nowhere to hide that this creature could not find her. Ailis knew that the way she knew her own breath.

"Tell me, child. Tell me what you are, that I should feel moved to see you again. That I must take note of you, and weave you into my plans."

"I . . . I don't know." The words were torn from her throat; the sensation of claws dragging along the flesh of her neck and mouth was so real she could almost taste the blood welling up and splashing her tongue.

"She is no one."

The relief Ailis felt at hearing Morgain's voice behind her was immeasurable. She would be happy to be no one, of no importance forever, if that figure would just stop staring at her. All Ailis wanted was to turn tail and hide behind Morgain's woolen skirts, like a child threatened by a snarling dog running home to its mother.

The shadow-figure's attention was not so much distracted as split. Ailis could feel the power of a cold wind, but it expanded to include the sorceress as well.

"You are a fool, Morgain. Would you jeopardize all that you have worked for? Delicate wheels are in motion, at your command. Do you hesitate now?"

"I am not hesitating," Morgain said, her voice still and hard, like the woman Ailis had first encountered, the cold and powerful sorceress Morgain Le Fay, scourge of Camelot. "All will be as we have planned it. Arthur will feel the weight of my hatred, and I shall have my revenge. The witch-child does not change that. The witch-child changes nothing you need be concerned with."

Ailis almost stopped breathing, willing them *both* to forget she existed.

"You think not. You know nothing. Fool mortal. Fool woman. Allow this, and all your plans will come to nothing. Arthur will gain the Grail, and you will fade from history, forgotten and unmourned."

The air in the hallway seemed to grow even colder, and Morgain drew herself up to her full height—a warrior-queen afraid of nothing, beholden to no one. Her face twisted in anger, the even white teeth suddenly showing like the fangs of the great cat she kept as a pet. "I am your hostess. I am she who called you to these shores. Forget that at your own peril."

Ailis still couldn't breathe. She didn't dare breathe. Warrior-queen or no, evil sorceress or no, couldn't Morgain feel how dangerous this stranger was? It was like keeping a dragon on a jeweled leash; fine until the dragon tired of the game and snapped the leash and devoured you in one bite.

"You know nothing of peril," the figure spat.

"I know *everything* of peril," Morgain spat back. "Do not push, Old One. I brought you to these shores, and I can still send you hence."

A hiss from the shadow-figure, a warm note of anger cutting through the cold wind, and when Ailis blinked, it was gone.

Morgain muttered something in a language Ailis did not know, but the girl could agree with the thought it conveyed, and sighed in relief.

Then Morgain let out a deep breath, and turned to face Ailis. Her expression was calm, controlled, her perfect features perfect once again.

"And now, witch-child, back to work."

In the face of that calm control, Ailis swallowed the questions she desperately wanted to ask, the salty tang of blood a reminder that there were things she did not want to be involved with any further, if she could possibly help it. This was a dangerous place. A bad place. Despite the contentment she had discovered here, a part of her mind still remembered that Morgain was an immense danger, an evil woman, the enemy of Arthur and Merlin, and therefore of Ailis as well.

Do not think on things you cannot change. There was no doubt that it was Morgain's voice, soothing the raw edges of Ailis's mind. *Focus on who and what you are, who and what you may become. That and that alone you may control.*

It was good advice. Ailis wrapped herself again in that soothing tone and took comfort in its words as the two went back up into the workroom and closed the heavy wooden door behind them.

* * *

"*This* is where Morgain is hiding?" Newt, remembering the glories of the Isle of Apples, was incredulous.

"According to the lodestone . . . yes." Gerard shrugged, as though to deny responsibility for the answer.

"Well, it's not much to speak of, is it?" Sir Caedor said. "Not that I was expecting Camelot in miniature, but I at least thought there would be streets."

In truth, the village barely earned that name; a double handful of wood and stone houses built not along any discernible row or road, but scattered as though by whim and chance along the shoreline. Narrow paths wound around each building, created not by hoof and wheel, but by human feet. Gerard could hear the faint chatter of voices—children, he determined—off to the left, but there were no adults to be seen. The sun was well-risen in the sky, however, so it was entirely likely that every adult in the village was called to work. Gerard didn't know anything about the patterns of coastal life; he had been born to fertile farmlands and was fostered in a rocky domain where livestock, not fish, were the main concern.

"All roads lead to . . . what?" Sir Caedor wondered out loud, tracing the direction with his gaze. "Down to the sea. And what is of such interest in the sea?"

"Their livelihood," Newt said in a tone of amazement. "This is a fishing village. Everyone here takes their living from the ocean."

"Information. We need more information," the knight went on, ignoring Newt entirely. "The lodestone sent us here, to a place from which we can travel no farther, so there must be an answer of some sort waiting for us. Let us go and inquire, if we can find a soul to speak with."

The two boys rode their horses forward, and followed Sir Caedor down one of the wider, more clearly defined paths, down a slight incline to where three larger square buildings partially blocked their view of the water down below.

"Do you know what you're going to say, to convince someone to let us borrow a boat?" Newt asked.

"I was thinking about invoking Arthur's name," Gerard said. "We are on his business, after all."

"You think they'll believe that?" They did have a parchment with the king's signature on it, the same one they had used to gain a room at the inn. Inns were used to that sort of thing, but the odds of anyone in this rough place being able to read were slim, at best. And even if they could, they would likely be disinclined to give over something as valuable as a boat to three strangers, so far from Camelot's immediate reach and reward.

"Well, we do have a knight with us," Gerard responded. "Maybe they'll be impressed by that."

"Optimist," Newt muttered, dire down to his toes. Gerard laughed for the first time in days.

He *was* optimistic, or at least optimistic in this regard, on this day, this hour. They were close, the lodestone had led them well, and he had confidence in Ailis. She was well. She would remain strong until they could rescue her. They could accomplish anything so long as they held together. Sir Caedor might not believe it, but Gerard knew Ailis; knew her better than anyone.

"You! Sirrah! Stop when I speak to you!"

"Oh, drat!" Newt said, and they both continued forward, too late to stop Sir Caedor from accosting a man walking toward them, away from the shoreline.

"Getcher hands off me," the man growled, then blanched at the sight of two more riders bearing down on him.

"Sir Caedor. Release him."

"He was insolent!"

"Release him." For just an instant, Gerard sounded like the king. So much so that Sir Caedor's hand released the man of its own accord, in an instinctive reflex. *Wow,* Gerard thought, but couldn't stop to enjoy the moment. Newt dismounted, holding Loyal's reins so that he stood off to Gerard's side. It was a planned move on Newt's part; not of a servant but as a well-treated companion of lesser social standing. With luck, that consideration would offset Sir Caedor's poor manners and reassure the man enough so that he would speak to Gerard without fear.

"I apologize," Gerard said now. "We have been riding for many days and we had hopes that you might be able to aid us."

The stranger looked at Gerard warily, glancing first at Sir Caedor, then at Newt, and then to Gerard again.

"With what?"

"We are in need of a guide to the home of Morgain Le Fay."

The villager stared up at them, his weathered face creased even more as he scowled. Then his mouth worked, and he spat a yellowish globule that hit Gerard on the leg.

The squire didn't flinch, not even when Sir Caedor pulled his sword from its scabbard, ready to slay the villager where he stood.

"I have offended?" Gerard asked, as mildly as he

could, while Newt moved to be ready to restrain Sir Caedor, if needed. How, Newt wasn't sure. But he would give Gerard time to ask whatever questions he needed to.

"You *are* offensive," the villager said. "You ride here, you grab, you demand, you would disturb the Lady Morgain—why? What business have you with her?"

"The king has sent us to parley with the Lady Morgain on matters of importance to him, and to her."

"Then the king should have sent you the means and direction on how to visit her," the old man said. "None here will convey you without her own request."

"But the king—"

"We have served the Lady Morgain's family for generations," the local said, his voice dripping scorn. "The family that *stayed* here, walked the sand, same as us. Not some bastard child gone off to warm a fancy chair down in the southlands."

Sir Caedor surged forward at the insult to the king, and even Newt jerked in reaction. But Gerard stayed them both with a glance and an upraised hand. Arthur had surely heard worse in his years.

"We have reason to believe that she would make us welcome on our arrival."

"Then she will send a way for you to make that arrival," the old man said. "'Tis not our place to make it happen."

They stared at each other, one pair of eyes lined and weighted but still bright, the other road-weary and shadowed. And in the end, it was Gerard who blinked and looked away, feeling the surge of Arthur's wisdom rising up inside him, even without the scar's itching.

"Let's go," Gerard said, finally. "Perhaps someone down in the village proper will be more open to discussion."

FIFTEEN

Ailis felt uneasy. Since the shadow-figure confronted her in the hallway, she had not slept well. She would wake confused and upset, memories of Camelot mixing with nightmares of a winged figure chasing her down endless whitewashed halls, calling her name, whispering something in her ear. Only the arrival each morning of Morgain, to escort Ailis to the tower that held her workroom, made everything make sense again. Morgain kept her safe. When she was working with the enchantress, learning new things, discovering parts of her that Merlin had only hinted about, that was when she felt balanced, alive and whole. Only then would the memories, and the nightmares, slip away.

"Do you know what to do?"

"Yes, Morgain," Ailis replied. "I know what to do."

"I won't be gone long." The sorceress hovered by the door, clearly torn between staying and going.

"I'm fine, Morgain. It's a simple assignment, no more difficult than remembering which side of the table to serve first, and in what order. I managed that by the time I was ten!"

The sorceress laughed, as Ailis had intended her to do, then finally left in a flurry of rich fabrics—finer than she usually wore to the workroom. She closed the door behind her and locked it from the outside. The sound of the magical bolt sliding into place should have made Ailis feel protected, safe. The shadow-figure could not reach her here.

But this morning, for some reason, the sensation of being tucked away behind that lock made Ailis feel restless, as if she had forgotten something, misplaced something.

Suddenly, the thought of comparing the ingredients of a wind-calming spell against the ingredients of a wind-calling spell seemed tedious and tiring. She pushed her stool back across the stone floor and looked around. She was bored. And she hadn't been told *not* to poke around. Not exactly.

A moment later she found herself not at the wooden worktable, with the two spells' ingredients neatly laid out, but standing in front of the far wall, which was draped with a heavy sailcloth cover. She wasn't sure why that cover fascinated her so, but she was learning to trust her instincts. Something she needed was behind there. But what was it?

A flutter of wings behind her made the girl jump. She turned and stared around the empty room. Nothing was there. Nothing at all.

Wings, again. A flutter of air, touching the feather braided into her dark red hair and brushing against her neck.

Find out what she's up to.

Ailis jumped again at Merlin's voice; the faint echo slipped into her mind on the tail end of a breeze, and then was gone again.

Merlin?

There was no response. Had the voice been real? Or was it merely her own imagination, colored by his memory? Ailis didn't know. But the temptation was irresistible: to discover something on her own, and not wait for Morgain—for anyone—to decide that she needed to know it.

She lifted the cloth, almost as though in a trance, feeling the heavy oiled fabric shift under her hands as she moved it aside. If she concentrated on it, that thought might somehow warn Morgain, bring her back unexpectedly. Ailis told herself: *Don't think. Don't trust your mind. Your mind lies to you. Trust your instincts. Trust your voices.*

"Oh."

Tacked to the wall was what seemed to be no more than an ordinary map. A map of the entire island—from the Scottish wilderness and the mountains of Gwynnedd, down to the southern lands and civilized Camelot, and across the waters to Brittany, where Sir Lancelot came from. Then Ailis saw small colored lights—magic, to glow so—hovering just above the surface of the map. Some were a pale blue, others dark red, while some shone cold steady white. They were scattered across the map. She blinked, and let her eyes refocus. Slowly, a pattern emerged, not so much through her eyes or her mind, but somewhere in between, in the same space where she could *feel* the magic that rested in both Morgain and Merlin.

The blue seemed to represent Arthur's men. His knights, landowners, common folk. The white were Morgain's allies. Fighters, farmers, and fisherfolk, hedge-witches and minor wizards—followers of the Old Ways who were unhappy with Arthur's embrace of the new God and the quest for the Christian Grail.

"Morgain wants to destroy the Quest." No great surprise there—that had been made plain from Morgain's very first move. But this was more than the sleep-spell. This involved other people. Warriors. Townspeople. People Arthur thought he could trust, many he thought were loyal subjects, all scattered along the routes to holy places, places a knight searching for a holy object might go. Morgain wanted more than the failure of the Quest, Ailis realized: She wanted the Grail to herself.

But what were those red spots? Try though she might, Ailis could not make that information come to her. The red lights remained a mystery. But clearly Morgain was planning something. That sleep-spell had not been her entire attack—only the first strike of her blade.

And Ailis was stuck here, unable to leave, unable to contact Merlin, unable to do anything, except keep on as she had been doing.

And really, Ailis thought, replacing the sailcloth cover, *what else should I be doing?*

You are a witch-child, a voice whispered to her from deep within her dreams. *Your place is near magic.* Morgain's voice? Or, as she was coming to suspect, the voice of the place, the magic in its very stones and water? It didn't matter. That comfortable sense of belonging was sliding back over her, wiping away the alarm and replacing it with the need to be back at her work.

This time, the flutter of wings against her neck was nothing more than the sea breeze coming in through the small window overhead.

When Morgain returned a short while later, Ailis was back on her stool, measuring the quantity of gossamer sand needed for each spell. Morgain didn't even glance at the covered wall before coming over to check on Ailis's progress.

"Excellent work," the sorceress praised, letting some of the tension fade from her face. Ailis could feel herself practically glowing under the older woman's approval.

So what if Morgain wanted to make trouble for Arthur? There was nothing Ailis could do about it for now, and it was none of her affair, anyway.

SIXTEEN

"Show me Morgain's home," Gerard uttered in frustration as they left the village. But the lodestone had done exactly that. The three were led to an almost completely hidden path that led around the town and up the rocky cliff. In the distance, out to the east, over cold gray water and under an equally gray sky, they could see the Orkneys. On the nearest of those islands, a stone-walled fortress rose from the ground as though thrust up from the earth itself; immovable, unshakable.

"That's it?"

"That's it," Newt said. "Unless Merlin's been having a joke on us all this time."

He sounded as bitter as Gerard felt. The villagers had not been welcoming. Just as the first man they encountered, many of the townsfolk refused to even speak to the strangers. Finally, Gerard had taken Sir Caedor and the horses away, leaving Newt alone to discover what he could, on foot. The little he had learned was that the first old man was right—no one would guide them.

"We will still need a boat if we try to go on our own." Sir Caedor sounded even less enthused about the prospect of travel over water than he had about travel over land.

"We should be able to hire a boat in the village," Newt said. Then he reconsidered, in light of their earlier reception. "Or maybe we'll have to borrow one without asking."

"Steal one?"

"Is it stealing if you return it when you're done?"

"Yes." Sir Caedor was definitive on that, as he was whenever he and Newt disagreed on anything. Which was almost always.

Newt shrugged. "Then we're stealing it. You have another idea?"

Sir Caedor clearly wanted to take Newt to task for insolence, but kept his lips firmly pressed together.

Gerard was thankful—he wasn't sure he was up to yet another round of peacekeeping, especially when he felt like pitching them both into a well and leaving them there.

Being the leader didn't mean leading so much as it meant balancing, Gerard decided, turning to look out over the water once again. He felt that strange warm touch inside again, like heated bathwater rising around his heart. He knew this had come from Arthur's blood-gift.

"Are you there, Ailis?" he asked quietly, touching Guinevere's token, the silver band that still rested on his arm. "Are you waiting for us to come and rescue you? We're almost there. Just hold on a little while longer." He heard Newt ride up alongside him, Loyal dancing a little as the smells of the sea reached his sensitive nostrils.

"So. We're going over there," Newt said quietly.

"That was always the plan. We just have to figure out how. Other than stealing a boat, that is."

"Oh, I said that just to choke him a little," Newt said dismissively. "About crossing the water, though—I think I have an idea how we can do it."

"Talk." Gerard went from distracted to focused, like a dog scenting a hare.

"Did you see, when we were down in the village, how the docks were laid out?"

Gerard leaned forward. He nodded as the other boy spoke, his hands painting a picture in the air.

*   *   *

Sir Caedor was accustomed to not being included in the conferences of his betters—his forte was battle, not strategy. But the way the two boys in his charge were huddled together stung nonetheless. Only the fact that the king and queen had tasked him with their safety kept him from taking their insults to heart. You had to let youngsters gain a little confidence, else they would forever be followers. Arthur was right about that. And it was clear from all signs that the young squire Gerard was being groomed for more than a follower, even if the boy wasn't aware of it yet. The way the squire had laid down the law back at the inn was proof that he had confidence in his own decisions and the ability to take risks. Caedor had been a squire before he was a knight, and he had heard plenty of older knights and warleaders scream when he did something wrong. He had trained raw youths—and this was not so different, for all that it required a more delicate touch. He understood now that Gerard, for all his tender years, was almost a man. And the stable boy, too, if far too prideful for his situation in life. So for now, Caedor sat back and let them have their head—until he saw something in the distance that made him frown in concern.

"Hmm." He rode forward, pushing his way into their consultation.

"What?" Gerard was clearly irritated at being interrupted, but Sir Caedor did not back down this time.

"I have not spent much time on the seas—I am no sailor—but it does not seem entirely . . . natural to me, for the waters to be behaving thus."

Gerard and Newt left off their discussion and looked to where Sir Caedor was pointing.

"Oh. Uh-oh."

"What in the name of Camelot is that?" Gerard asked.

"I don't know," Sir Caedor replied. "But I don't like it."

They turned their horses along the cliff-side path for a better view, and watched as the surface of the ocean frothed and foamed out beyond where the normal whitecaps were forming on top of the ever-rolling waves. It looked almost as though the water was boiling, but just in that one location.

"It couldn't be natural?" Newt asked. "Some kind

of storm front moving in? Or maybe a waterspout. One of the knights in Camelot was telling stories of those at the Quest banquet, how they form out of nowhere. You can't see them until they're almost right on you, and then it's too late. . . ."

"It might be," Gerard said. "Do you want to risk it being totally unrelated to us, or our mission, this close to Morgain's home?"

Newt didn't. "So, what . . . we wait it out?"

"If it's natural, it should wax and wane, as all storms do. If it's not—"

"It is not," Sir Caedor said, still watching the waters. His skin had turned an ashen gray, and his right hand was clenching and unclenching on the reins of his horse. "We need to get back to the village. They may not like us, but if this is something dangerous, they need to be warned."

In accord, they started back down the path, moving as swiftly as they could without risking the horses' safety on the uneven ground. The path wound, serpentine, and they had their backs to the ocean for several yards. When they faced the ocean again, the waters had ceased foaming.

Instead, a long wake formed behind the giant head of a beast rising from the ocean's surface, coming directly at them. From the size of its head, and the probable depth of the water, Gerard thought the thing might be as tall as Camelot itself.

"God and the saints have mercy," Sir Caedor muttered. The two boys were struck mute. The beast was coming for them, and coming fast.

"Let the horses go," Gerard said suddenly.

"What?" Newt managed to take his eyes off the approaching beast long enough to give Gerard a blank stare. Sir Caedor, however, saw where Gerard was going with that thought. He dropped out of his saddle with surprising agility, swinging an armor-clad leg over as though it weighed nothing, and dropping to the ground even as he was tying the reins up so the horse would not stumble over them and break its neck.

"A distraction," he said. "Excellent. With luck, when it gets to shore, the creature will go for the easy food and leave us be."

Gerard shrugged an apology at Newt's accusing look and followed suit. Newt looked as though he might resist, but then did the same for Loyal.

"Sorry, boy," he said, resting his palm against the horse's muscled neck. As much as he loved his charges, Gerard was right. It wasn't much of a chance, but it was the only one they had. People before animals, and no room for sentimentality.

With a hard, openhanded slap, he startled Loyal into a dash of speed, made easier by the lack of rider on his back. The other two horses and the mule, likewise encouraged, took off up the steep path after him.

The sea-beast's snake-like head swiveled to watch the animals run. For a long moment, all three humans held their breath, praying that the ruse would work. Then, with a low moan, the serpent turned its attention back to the smaller prey, resuming its gliding approach through the deep water toward the rocky shoreline.

"It's intelligent," Sir Caedor said, in a tone of total disbelief. "To go after smaller prey, when it's that size . . ."

"It's not interested in horses. It wants humans. Someone sent it after us," Gerard said flatly. "And no fair guessing who."

"Morgain. Perfect. We're dead." Newt wasn't whining, only stating a cold, dry fact as he watched the beast reach the shore and emerge onto the rocky soil.

The beast was like nothing any of them had ever

seen before. One quick glance at Sir Caedor confirmed that he was at a loss as well. Sinewy and sleek, like a sea-monster, it nonetheless moved easily on land, propelled by a dozen thick legs with wide paddle-like paws.

Propelled quickly, Newt realized. Up the steep cliff-side trail directly toward them.

"Run!" Newt urged his companions, turning to take his own advice.

"Where?" Sir Caedor stood tall, drawing his sword. "Where will you go that it cannot reach you?"

The knight had a point. They were a long distance from the village, and they did not want to lead the beast there, to unprotected fisherfolk, no matter how unfriendly. Morgain might have sent it after them, but there was no assurance that it could tell one two-legged figure from another. Hiding was out, as well. The nearest rocks would not have hidden them all. The beast was far taller than any of the scrub-trees they might climb, even if it hadn't been easy to knock those trees down and make a mouthful of them.

Newt noted, even in his fear, that the thing didn't have much of a mouth, just a narrow slit with a pair of fangs hanging over either side.

And then the serpent-beast's mouth opened. And kept opening, its jaws unhinging until it could have swallowed Newt *and* Loyal whole, and still had room for a small dog or two.

"We need to jump."

Gerard said it in such a matter-of-fact voice that it took Newt a moment to process what he had heard.

"Jump?" All three of them risked a glance over the cliffs. It wasn't all that far, as suicidal leaps from cliffs went. And the rocks below weren't all that sharp, for the jagged-edged shards that they were. Odds were they might even survive the attempt—at least one of them.

"And what if there's another one of those beasties in the surf?"

Gerard looked at Newt and flashed him a totally unconvincing grin. "Then you don't have to explain to the stable master how you lost yet another pack mule."

"I'm not jumping down there! I'm not jumping anywhere!"

"You have a better suggestion?"

"I want to die on land!"

"I don't want to die at all!" Gerard retorted.

"Neither of you will die today," Sir Caedor said grimly. He had been watching the sea-beast as it moved farther up the trail, and his sword-tip was slowly tracking its movements. His face under his helm was tense, but his shoulders were relaxed, his one-handed grip on the hilt of his weapon steady.

"Sir Caedor . . ." Gerard stepped forward, his hand going to his own sword, still sheathed at his side.

"I swore an oath to bring you boys to your destination safely. I intend to keep that vow." The tired, irritated traveler was gone. In his place stood the man Sir Caedor had been a decade before, when he stood with Arthur and helped to drive the darkness from their isle. The light of battle was in his eyes, and his lips pulled back in a truly terrifying grin.

"Sir—" Gerard started to protest again, but the older man cut him off.

"Go, boys."

When they simply stood there staring at him, he shoved his free arm back and hit Gerard square in the chest with full force. "Go!"

The squire staggered back, his arms windmilling slightly, reaching for anything that might stop his fall. Unfortunately, the only thing available to grab was Newt. Unprepared for the hand snagging his sleeve, Newt fell backward as well. Suddenly the air was whistling past their ears, mingling with the sound of Sir Caedor shouting his battle cry, a clear "come and take me, if you can" taunt to the sea-beast.

And then they each hit the ice-cold water with a sharp and terrifying slap, and everything went dark.

*   *   *

Newt resurfaced into achingly crisp air, with a waterlogged Gerard still clutching his tunic. Holding his friend's head above water, he set out in slow, awkward strokes, heading toward the nearest islet. He didn't think, didn't wonder, didn't do anything except swim, lugging his burden with a dogged single-mindedness until he felt something bump under his legs and he was able to stand for a moment. He let go of his companion and collapsed to his knees. Newt discovered that the surface under him was slippery rock, and that the wavelets only came to his shoulder. They had made it to the islet.

"Come on, come on," he encouraged himself, slogging across the last distance until they were actually on solid, barren land.

He heaved Gerard out of the water and examined him. Gerard had a set of nasty bruises on his face that were already turning a sort of greenish-purple, and there were scrapes and cuts everywhere his skin was exposed. Newt suspected, from the sting of salt water everywhere, that he looked much the same. But Gerard's chest still moved up and down, slowly, as he breathed, and his color was not all that much paler than usual. So nobody was dead.

Yet.

With that thought, Newt's gaze was drawn across the narrow channel of water—it had seemed so much wider when he was swimming it—to the cliffs they had just fallen from.

Sir Caedor was barely visible, dwarfed by the monster that reared four or five times his height over him. But the sunlight glinted on his blade as it swung and made contact. The serpent-monster swiped at him in return, but its paddle-legs were less useful on land than they might have been in the water, and the sword had clearly made it wary.

Perhaps once the knight was able to take down the beast, they could regroup and find a way to set out for Morgain's island. For the first time since their departure from Camelot, Newt started to feel some real optimism. Caedor might not be able to defeat that beast, but he should be able to use his much smaller size to elude it—the thing was ungainly, like the oliphants Newt had heard of.

Sir Caedor really could prevail. Newt might not like the man personally, but Arthur's knowledge had flowed into him enough. He was able to have trust, at least while they weren't actively arguing with each other.

"Urrrgggle."

Newt looked down to see Gerard stirring slightly, flinching as his hand came up to touch his forehead where the bruising was the worst. "Welcome back to the Land of the Not-Dead," he said, then turned back to watch the battle on the cliff. "Careful, careful . . ."

"We fell."

"You were pushed, I was pulled," Newt corrected.

"I'm going to kill him," Gerard said with feeling, discovering that his sword had come out of its scabbard when they fell. It was now lost somewhere in the waves.

"You may not get the chance," Newt said, standing abruptly as the tenor of the fight changed, visible even at this distance. The sea-beast swooped and swerved, trying to drive Sir Caedor over the cliff and into the waters where the beast would have a clear advantage.

The knight sidestepped the swerve at the last minute, dancing out of harm's way and—

"No!" Newt yelled, helpless, as the knight's actions took him too close to the monster. Its great head swung down, great jaws opening until they took Caedor's upper body between its hideous lips and closed down with a snap that Newt could almost swear he heard from where he stood.

"No," Newt said again. "No, oh, no."

The two of them waited, one sprawled awkwardly on the rocks, the other standing. They watched as the serpent reared back again, as though looking for further prey, then coiled in on itself and dove over the cliff, disappearing into the cold gray depths without further fuss.

"Dear God," Gerard said, crossing himself. It was the first time Newt could remember ever seeing the squire do that. Had he been so inclined, Newt might have done the same, but instead he simply bowed his head for a moment, sending a prayer that Sir Caedor's soul find peace in whatever afterlife he found.

"Do you think . . . it's waiting? Looking for us?" Newt asked, shivering in a way that had absolutely nothing to do with their recent immersion in the cold water.

"No. I think it was sent to kill humans with swords," Gerard said, slowly sitting up with a painful grimace. "It did that, and it left. I'd wager everything on it."

"You're going to have to," Newt said, trying to focus on the immediate problem rather than what they had just seen. "Now that Sir Caedor's gone, it's up to us. And if we're going to finish this mission— if Sir Caedor's death is going to mean anything— we're going to have to swim back through that water, to shore."

SEVENTEEN

Their return to the village was much less impressive than their first visit, trudging on foot with no horses, no mule, and no knight. Their clothing and hair was still damp from their nerve-racking swim back to shore, during which they had thankfully been unmolested by anything more aggressive than a school of inquisitive fish.

The trek was a quiet one, neither boy feeling much urge to talk, with the memory of Sir Caedor's death still raw in their minds. Gerard started to say something when they came around the bend in the path and saw the village in front of them, but his thoughts were too jumbled to speak out loud just yet. Newt had taken the queen's token off his arm and was holding it in his hand, his thumb stroking the cool metal absently.

They had seen death before, from battle and illness and old age. This was different. This was death in order that they might live. This was death with obligation.

It aged you, somehow. They both felt the weight of Caedor's act in their bones. And neither Merlin's cunning nor Arthur's wisdom were coming forward to help them through it.

Maybe, Newt thought, that was the whole point. Maybe wisdom was knowing that nothing helped you deal with that. You just had to get up and go on.

They were back at the village almost before they realized it. The village faced the ocean in a half-circle, with the most important-looking buildings nearest the shore. One long dock stretched out into the water, like a finger testing the mood of the waves.

A deep-hulled boat was tied up to the dock, and workers were carrying bales of fabric up a ramp, where they were brought into the hold for storage. The two boys found a spot behind a pile of slatted boxes that smelled like dried beef where they could see without being seen.

"That boat's too small to go anywhere far," Newt said. "Odds are it's a local delivery."

"Local as in Lady Morgain's island?" Gerard

raised an eyebrow and looked at the boat more carefully. "Maybe. She's the only one who would be ordering that many supplies, certainly. It's a risk, though."

Newt snorted. "Because everything else we've done so far has been a certainty?" He had a point. "What does the lodestone say?"

Gerard felt for it and wrapped his fingers around the gray stone, but it remained still and cool under his hand. "Nothing."

"Great." Newt looked over the scene again, counting how many workers were loading and unloading, how they were dressed, and how much attention they paid to the surrounding area. "My gut still says this is the only way in. We know that they owe their allegiance to Morgain before Arthur—Sir Caedor was right about that. So just asking to be taken on board isn't going to do us any good."

"It might get us on that ship, but not in a way that will be useful," Gerard agreed.

"Boat, not ship."

"Whatever. How do we sneak on board?"

"Like this."

Newt pushed the silver band up his arm and replaced his sleeve over it. Then he reached over and grabbed a rough-hewn sack and hefted it over his shoulder so that it hid his face from casual observation without blocking his own ability to see where he was going. He stood up and walked out from behind the bales and into the crush of villagers without waiting to see if Gerard was joining him.

"Idiot!" Gerard muttered, but covered his own band, grabbed a sack of his own, and followed.

"Walk slower," Newt said when Gerard caught up with him. "Casual, like you really don't care if you get where you're going 'cause you know you're going to."

"That makes absolutely no sense."

"Trust me."

The two of them moved up the ramp onto the boat, Gerard having to duck under a timber pole that was being swung around and raised in one smooth movement. He recovered in time to see Newt moving toward the hold, where materials were being deposited.

"Breakables," Newt said to the man reaching up to take the sack from him. "My head if I don't set it down m'self."

Gerard blinked. He knew it was Newt's voice. He saw Newt's lips moving as the words were spoken. And yet, somehow, it didn't sound like Newt at all. The tones were broader, rougher, a little deeper—much closer to the way the other villagers sounded, now that he thought about it.

Not trusting himself to manage the same trick, Gerard lengthened his stride to catch up with Newt, following him down the ladder into the hold with his own sack.

The ladder was short and the hold was dark. They had to wait a moment for their eyes to adjust.

"Over there," a voice told them, and Gerard jumped. But the clerk, having given them directions, was more interested in ordering the ongoing flow of boxes. He turned his back and paid them no more attention.

Newt set his sack down carefully between two boxes, and, without pausing, disappeared into the deeper shadows of the hold. Gerard did the same, feeling far too exposed despite the fact that he knew, intellectually, that if he could not see Newt, then no one would be able to see him, either.

A tug on his arm guided him down to the floor, where Newt was already settled, sitting cross-legged with his back against the wall.

And there, barely breathing for fear of being

overheard by the workers still loading and counting off boxes, they waited.

Eventually, the last box was sent down and marked off. The clerk finalized his accounting and climbed up the ladder. He secured the trapdoor firmly behind him.

The entire hold was plunged into total darkness.

"It worked." Newt sounded far too surprised for Gerard's peace of mind.

"Not yet, it hasn't. We still have to get there. And get off the boat without being seen. And then—"

"You can't ever accept a moment for what it is, can you?"

"In other words, you have no idea how we're going to manage any of that, either, do you?"

"The same way we got on, only in reverse," Newt said matter-of-factly.

"And getting off the island again, once we find Ailis?"

"I haven't the faintest idea," Newt admitted. "We'll figure something out." Gerard sensed Newt shrugging. "That's assuming Morgain doesn't kill us in the process. Or turn us into snails. Or . . ."

"I get the point," Gerard said. There was something being shouted outside, and a sudden lurch around them. The ropes had just been cast off. They were under way. He crossed his arms over his knees, rested his chin on his arms, and did the only thing he could do.

He went to sleep.

*   *   *

Arthur paced at the far end of the room, dictating a letter to be taken to the Marcher Lords who had threatened to rebel, discussing further terms of their parley, but Merlin could not let it distract him. Not when he was . . . almost . . . there. . . .

Ailis. Ailis. Drat it, child. Pay attention!

For an instant he thought he could almost feel the girl-child, like seeing a light flicker in the distance, through trees, but then it was gone, and Morgain's protections fell between them again. The enchanter sighed, knuckling his eyes and sitting back in his wooden chair.

"I'm sorry, sire," he said, speaking just loudly enough for his king to hear him. "The barriers . . . I felt them slip for an instant, but I could not reach through."

Arthur stopped long enough to come over and place a gentle hand on the enchanter's shoulder.

"Keep trying. If we can reach her, we can tell her what to look for and what to tell us. It's bad enough to discover Morgain's hand in this trouble along the northern borders, but what else might she be stirring?" The king continued, "And let Ailis know that help is on its way. So she can focus on learning Morgain's secrets, not escaping."

Merlin frowned, his concern for the child warring with his understanding of what was necessary. You used the weapons you had on hand. "Yes, sire."

Taking a deep breath, Merlin slid back into his trance. *Ailis! Be strong! We will not desert you. Strength is coming.*

He hoped.

EIGHTEEN

"Morgain?"

"Yes, witch-child?"

By now, Ailis had accustomed herself to Morgain's nickname for her. In time, she suspected that she might begin to think that it was her given name. Sleep last night had been filled with dreams of people calling for her, voices shouting each other down, pulling at her in a hundred different directions until she woke feeling exhausted, as though she had single-handedly served a midwinter feast. When Ailis woke at last, she hadn't been quite sure where she was or even who she was exactly. A hot bath and some herbal tea had soothed her body and sharpened her mind, but she was still feeling a little off-center and confused. She didn't like feeling confused. You couldn't be confused around Morgain. It was too dangerous.

"You had a question?" the sorceress prompted her.

Ailis pulled on her braid and smoothed the feather she now worked into her hair every morning. It was her talisman. It reminded her of dreams of flying, of dreams of magic under her own control. "Why did you put that sleep-spell on Camelot?"

Mixing a floury substance into a dark green liquid that simmered pleasantly, filling the workroom with the scent of pine and brine, Morgain stopped what she was doing and looked at Ailis in surprise.

"Why do *you* think I put that spell on Camelot?"

That had been the pattern for the past few days. Ailis would ask a question and Morgain would repeat it back to her. It would have been infuriating, except for the echo of Merlin's own eccentric speech patterns that made it somehow comforting as well. Were all magic users like that? Or was it simply Merlin's influence on Morgain long ago? Ailis didn't know.

"Some say that it's because you're evil. That you don't need any other reason."

"Is that what you think?" Morgain went back to her blending, as though the answer was of no importance at all.

The now-familiar space of the workroom gave Ailis courage to press on. "I think you have a reason. But it's not just because you're evil. I'm not . . . I'm not really sure that you are. Evil, I mean."

There. It was said.

That got a laugh out of Morgain; a real one, full-bodied and full of surprised delight.

"Oh, I'm evil, witch-child. Never mistake that. By the standards of those who raised you, I'm perhaps the most evil soul of all."

"By their standards?" Ailis repeated, confused.

"Mmmm. That is something I learned very early on, Ailis." The fact that Morgain used her real name made the girl pay closer attention. "Do not blindly accept the word of anyone who would tell you how things *must* be. Question, witch-child. Question especially those who would define 'evil' for you."

Ailis felt as though an entire hive of bees had moved into her head, buzzing and stinging in her brain. Morgain was trying to confuse her, make her question up and down, good and bad, right and wrong. It was her dream all over again—only Morgain's voice was blending with her own, until she wasn't sure where one ended and the other began, and the other voices were silent, gone away.

Right was right, and wrong was wrong. Evil was always evil. Wasn't it? The sense of clarity she always had with Morgain was gone, destroyed by her own question.

If evil wasn't always evil . . .

Ailis frowned, shook her head, looked at Morgain, then looked back down at the simple paste the sorceress had set her to mixing. Yellow and red swirled together to create, Morgain said, a potion that would aid in sleep. Sleep—or, in a certain dosage, death. A starter spell for a witch-child to do on her own. Nothing that could not be accomplished by herbals, but herbal mixtures often went bad quickly or lost their potency.

How easy, to turn helpful into harmful. Ailis could see that. How easy would it also be, then, to turn . . . good into evil?

Ailis wasn't naïve; you couldn't live in Camelot without seeing how the world worked. It would be useful for Morgain to have an ally, however low, in Camelot. The isolation, the treats, the fearsome figure—the sorceress could be trying to confuse her thinking, make her sympathetic to Morgain's cause, turn her loyalties . . . and then allow her to return home. And then, someday, when others had perhaps forgotten that she had once been prisoner of the sorceress, she could . . .

There, Ailis's imagination failed her. She could not imagine a single thing that Morgain might need her for, in the heart of Camelot. How could Ailis even assume that anyone would ever trust her after all this.

For all she knew, they had abandoned her, thought or even hoped she was dead.

Merlin! She tried to shout with her mind. *Merlin, help me!*

The only voice in her head now was her own.

"Why . . ." She paused, then rephrased her question, not even sure what she was going to say until she voiced it. "What did they say *must* be, that you believed them?"

For a long time, Ailis thought that Morgain was not going to answer her.

"When I was a child, my mother seemed a terribly powerful woman. Within our home, her word and her wish was law. But when my father died, Uther the King decided that my mother would be his bride. There was nothing she could do to stop him. Arthur came of that union. A boy. And because he was a boy, all the power and the glory went to him.

Not to the girl-children my mother had borne before. Not to the ones with the true power, the magic, the Old Ways in their blood. My sisters and I were simply not important.

"I was not born to live that way, witch-child. And neither were you." Morgain lifted her head as though listening to something, like alert dogs in a kennel, and stared at her for a moment. "Come with me."

Ailis practically had to run in order to keep up, for all that Morgain seemed to glide in exactly the same way the dance master had insisted upon, ages and ages ago back in Camelot. When the sorceress did it, the movements seemed graceful and deadly, not silly.

They went down the stairs, across the jointed walkway where Morgain's worktower connected to the rest of the fortress, and down a hallway that Ailis had never seen before. By now, the building's confusing layout had a strange familiarity to it, as though someone had burned the knowledge of every room into her bones. She knew where Sir Tawny would have room to spread his wings, and where she could go to sit and listen to the silence within the stones, should she so desire it. The magic of the undersea room was hers for the using now, and half a dozen other chambers besides.

A door appeared in the wall in front of them, and, without hesitating, Morgain put her left hand up, palm flat, and pushed against it while making a complicated gesture with her right hand held down around her hip. Ailis managed to watch both hands, but only barely—she was pretty sure that she had missed something in that right-hand gesture.

The stone door slid back, the same way Morgain's workroom doorway had, and the sorceress gently pushed Ailis through.

The last time Ailis had gone through a magically appearing doorway, it had taken her to and from the Isle of Apples, Morgain's home in the otherworld. So it was with relief that she realized that they had merely stepped outside the confines of the fortress and were now standing on the external walls, overlooking the village Ailis had only seen through windows. Beyond that, the ocean foamed gray-blue across to the mainland, where the waters crashed against the rocky shore.

"Beautiful, isn't it?"

Personally, Ailis thought it was barren and depressing and cold.

"Look into the water, witch-child. Look deep."

Ailis didn't bother to protest that the water was

too far away. Morgain would not ask something Ailis could not do. It was up to Ailis to discover *how* to do it.

Letting her mind float like the thick gray clouds overhead, Ailis focused on a cliff off in the distance, one that seemed to echo with a magical residue, resting her eyes on it until everything blurred, the same way she had looked at the map days ago. Then she let her gaze drift down into the deep, cold waters, down past the great schools of baitfish flickering like a single hungry beast, down farther to where the currents swirled and shoved against each other.

"Do you feel it, witch-child?"

Ailis nodded, her face a blank mask, the rest of her was out there in the swirling waters. It was like being back in the water-room, only more real. More *intense*.

"Take it. Take what you feel. Shape it. Fold it between your hands. Feel the power that resides within the water. Take it."

The wind stirred the feather braided into her hair, but did not so much as ruffle her clothing.

"It's too much," Ailis protested.

"Too much for a mortal frame, yes. It's not meant to run in your blood-filled body. But you can move it. Manipulate it."

"Move things with it?"

"Exactly!" Morgain's voice was pleased. Ailis could feel her chest swell with pride at having impressed her teacher so. "There's a ship out there coming from the mainland. Good sailors, all of them. My sailors. Shall we test them? Push their ship. Push it to their limits."

Ailis found the ship without difficulty—it was the only solid object on the damp seascape—and *shoved* the gathered force of the ocean against its wooden sides.

The wood shivered and rocked low in the waters. Ailis was amazed at how easy it was.

"Again," Morgain's voice encouraged her. *"Again."*

* * *

"Are you all right?"

"Yeah. Just a little . . . now I know why Sir Caedor didn't like boats." Newt wiped his mouth with the back of his hand, and took the waterskin from Gerard. He rinsed his mouth and spat the water out onto the floor of the hold. It was disgusting. He hadn't made a mess like that since he was ill as a child, but he did feel better.

"Come on, then." The sounds and feel of the boat

had begun to change, from the near-panic of the sudden storm to a more measured flurry of feet and voices, indicating that they were hopefully approaching Morgain's island stronghold.

The plan was to try and blend in with the workers unloading materials, the same way they had gotten themselves on board. The problem was that Morgain was bound to have her own people meeting the boat. "It's what *I* would do," Gerard had said.

"Not a huge presence," Newt had agreed. "Just one, maybe two people, to make sure the faces are all familiar and that nobody goes anywhere they're not supposed to be."

"Are we sure this is the right place?" Newt asked, just before he stuck his head up out of the hold.

"A little late to be worrying about that now, isn't it?" Gerard retorted, waiting at the base of the ladder.

"Check the lodestone."

"Against what?" But even as he protested, Gerard was reaching for the stone around his neck, drawing it up and out into the open. "All right," he said to it. "Are we in the right place?"

The stone seemed to shimmer slightly, and then burst into a handful of fine gray powder.

"Right." Gerard wiped powder off his nose and shook out his hair, spitting at the dry taste in his mouth. "Any other brilliant questions?"

Gerard and Newt mingled with the sailors unloading the boxes until they were able to work their way to the gangway. They were both work-hardened enough to pass, so long as no one looked too closely, but Newt's clothing was still closer in style; even the vomit stains added a touch of reality that Gerard's travel gear lacked, being of higher quality material than the average worker on that vessel could ever afford.

The dock was a sturdier structure than the one in the village, better made and better maintained, but for all that, it was still a simple wooden dock— nothing that would seem out of place in any port. Certainly not anything they might have expected, remembering the glimmer and shine of Morgain's abode on the mystical Isle of Apples.

Then again, the Isle of Apples had housed only Morgain and her great black cat, as far as anyone knew. This small, rock-crusted island seemed to be home to many more people, based on the number of souls coming down to meet the boat, waving and calling out greetings.

"Your first trip?" a sailor said to Newt, handing him the end of a rope and clearly expecting him to know what to do with it.

Newt merely nodded, watching the other man start to pull. His ability to mimic accents was best saved for emergencies—he had no confidence in how long he might be able to fool the locals.

"Nothin' to it," the man went on. "Towson's a fair master, a'long as you do your share a' the work and don't shirk off. Here from Glandis?"

"South," Newt said, not sure where Glandis was. "Hoping to get some skills, bring 'em home."

The answer seemed to satisfy the man's limited curiosity. "As I said, don't shirk and you'll do fine."

Newt suspected that sneaking off the moment he had a chance was going to qualify as shirking. Since he had no desire to bring home anything except Ailis, it didn't exactly depress him. He put his weight into pulling the rope as well, bringing them smoothly alongside the dock, which they hit with a solid thud of wood against wood.

"Welcome, and well come," one of the men on the dock said, all smiles. "In peaceful intent, and in peaceful depart. And good to see you, *White Lady*."

That speech gave Newt pause—the wording was

formal enough, and odd enough, to be the makings of a spell. But since he and Gerard had peaceful intent—they just wanted to get Ailis, not harm Morgain—he suspected that it would be safe enough to try and leave the boat. He hoped, especially since there wasn't any way to let Gerard know, not without raising suspicions. One newcomer might be normal enough. Two, especially two who knew each other, would be a different matter.

It took almost the entire afternoon to unload the boat, and by the end Newt wasn't sure he had the strength to walk away from the dock, much less do anything more strenuous. When the last box was piled onto the back of the last wagon, and the last crack of reins and creak of wheels had sounded, he joined the other workers, both local and shipboard, in collapsing on the dock, passing waterskins and eating strips of dried meat.

"*Psst.*"

Newt lifted his head to see a figure in a dirty leather apron gesturing to him. It took a long moment before the dirt-smudged figure, with fair hair slicked back and darkened, resolved into the familiar features of Gerard.

"Wha?"

"Come on!"

Newt found the energy to get to his feet. He walked away slowly, so as not to attract any attention. But it seemed as though the rest of the crew was just as exhausted as he was.

"Where have you—"

"I was sent to get the meats. Borrowed this apron from the butcher's apprentice. Here." He handed Newt a similar garment. "They were slaughtering today. They're delivering all over the island now. Nobody will look twice at us."

"Nice," Newt said in appreciation, even as he wrinkled his nose at the smell. Dogs and horses were clean, compared to cattle. But he put the apron on and followed Gerard up the stone-paved road, following the trail the wagons had taken. Straight up to the great fortress they had first seen from the cliff, where Morgain—and Ailis—waited.

NINETEEN

"Why aren't there any protections?" Newt wondered out loud.

"How do we know there aren't?"

"Don't say things like that. It makes my stomach hurt."

They had just walked under the great stone-gated entrance to the keep. Other than a glance from a pair of lightly armed guards, nobody had taken any notice of them whatsoever. It was making Gerard nervous. Newt had started at nervous, and was about to move into panic.

"She knows we're coming." Newt had begun to sweat, although the eve was cool and there was still a breeze coming off the shoreline, up the rocky hill.

Gerard reached up to touch Guinevere's silver token, replaced on his arm once they were far enough away from the boat and its crew for it to be safe to wear. It was silly, but it gave him strength, somehow. He supposed that was the point of tokens. They weren't magical, not the way Merlin's blood-gift was, but the reminder that someone had faith in him, believed in him, was power of another sort. "How?" he asked Newt, returning to the conversation as they kept moving forward. If he could keep Newt talking, maybe he'd be able to remain just calm enough.

"Um, she's a sorceress?" Newt retorted, his gaze darting back and forth as though expecting something to jump out of them from thin air.

An unarguable point that did not do much to calm his nerves. But he kept walking. "She's not invincible. We beat her before."

Newt snorted. "She let us win before."

That was the harsh truth. If Morgain had chosen to use magic against them in their last conflict, they would have been dead; Camelot would have been defeated. She pulled back, and only resorted to magical attack at the last moment, as they fled through the gateway to Camelot.

Gerard suspected then what he was convinced of now; that Morgain had some long-term plan involving Arthur and the Quest. Killing children under his protection would add an element of risk she couldn't afford. It was what had kept him optimistic about Ailis's fate, especially when Merlin seemed to believe the same thing about Morgain's intent.

He wasn't sure if that was reassuring or not. He thought probably not.

Meanwhile, Newt described the speech he had overheard that sounded like a spell. Gerard had agreed that it was probably a basic defense against would-be attackers.

"If they do that spell on every ship that comes in, and the only way to come in is either by boat, or magic, then so long as you don't come in via magic they know you're not a threat, and if you do come in via magic, if you're not invited, odds are you're a threat."

"I wonder why Merlin doesn't teach us a spell like that."

"Because there are too many ways to get at Camelot," Gerard said, bringing himself back to the conversation at hand with mild frustration. "An island is easier to protect, because you have the water as an ally."

Merlin had said that Morgain would be overconfident. She was arrogant enough to go to Camelot herself. How much more prideful, how much more overconfident, would she be in her own home? Even if she did sense them coming, she would believe they were no real threat to her here. That was the hope, anyway. Without hope, they should just lay down here and wait to die.

Sir Caedor had already died. But he had met it head-on, not waiting like a sheep.

They passed through the courtyard, a huge open space with buildings on three sides and the great gate behind them. Now they had to decide where to go.

"The lodestone would have been helpful now," Newt grumbled.

"Well, we don't have it. Time to go on ordinary instinct and common sense."

"Ordinary and common, I've got," Newt said. "All right. Young girl, troublemaker, prisoner, but not someone you want to keep in the dungeon."

"How do you know she wouldn't—"

"Like you said. Instinct. Common sense. If she's kept Ailis alive, she's keeping her . . . not in the dungeon. Somewhere . . . secure, but not uncomfortable. Like a hostage."

"Exactly like a hostage," Gerard said. "What did Arthur do when we had those princelings last year?" He was speaking to himself, not expecting Newt to have paid any attention to the dealings of the court. "A high room, something with a view, maybe. Where there's limited access but not a sense of punishment, as such."

"Like a tower." There were three towers in the fortress, two short and somewhat stubby, and the third tall and elongated.

"Maybe. But . . ." Newt looked around, under the guise of being an awestruck butcher's apprentice traveling somewhere he had never been. "Or there."

Newt jerked his chin to indicate a section between the two shorter towers, a single layer suspended in midair that overhung the courtyard where they stood. There were no windows along its length, not even any slits where bowmen might stand defensively, as might be expected in such a structure.

It looked wide enough to contain rooms, rather than merely being a corridor. If it did—even if it didn't—it was a good place to start.

The only problem, they discovered, was getting to where they thought they wanted to go. They had found the doorway easily enough; there were four entrances to the fortress, one placed in each corner of the keep, each with its own design on the arch over the door and a single guard who watched them with oddly slanted green eyes as they passed, but did not challenge them. Once inside, things became more difficult.

"No wonder she doesn't have more guards," Newt said in disgust. "She doesn't need them. This place is a maze!"

"A maze is easy to get around in," Gerard disagreed. "It's all just a question of figuring out how it was designed." But he was frustrated as well as nervous, now, and while the seasickness had worn off, it was replaced by the itchy feeling between his shoulder blades that he always got just before the start of a practice tourney. It felt like someone was watching him, studying him, trying to determine the best way to knock him off his horse. Morgain? Or . . .

"This place . . . this place wasn't designed. It's alive."

Newt swallowed hard. "Was that supposed to make me feel better? Because it didn't."

They had been walking forever, it seemed, down a hallway carpeted with a thick green rug that ran its entire length. There were doors set into the cream-colored stone walls. They checked the unlocked doors that led into chambers of various sizes and furnishings, but all were empty with no signs of recent occupancy.

"At least we haven't found any skeletons of strangers who wandered in and walked until they died."

"This is no time to develop a sense of humor," Gerard said.

Newt blinked. "Who said I was joking?" Then he grinned, more out of stress than actual mirth.

"Hah."

"Seriously, though," Newt said. "We could do this for days."

"What do you suggest then? If we still had the lodestone—"

"It wouldn't do us any good. It wasn't taking us to Ailis. It was taking us to Morgain's home. Well, here it is and here we are. Besides, do you really think any of Merlin's magic is going to function accurately inside Morgain's own lair? Not without Merlin along to work it, and there's no way he could have gotten onto this island."

A fact the enchanter had to have been aware of. "Otherwise occupied" had been a way of saying "I'm sending you where I can't go." Merlin was a master of not quite lying.

"So what do you suggest?" he asked Newt. The other boy had more experience being sneaky than he did. Gerard was pretty sure about that.

"Ever lose anyone in the woods?"

"No," Gerard said, giving him a look that clearly questioned if the other boy had gone frothing mad.

"You don't chase after them, that just gets you both lost. You let them come to you." Newt stopped and planted his feet, raising his hands to his mouth and cupping them around his mouth. Taking a deep breath, he bellowed: "Ailis! Ailis, we're here!"

The hallway echoed with his words, the stone bouncing them back, loud enough to make them both flinch.

"You are *insane*!" Gerard turned and waved his arms at Newt in his agitation, his face flushing pink. "Morgain—"

"You would rather wander around forever without a clue? Besides, I doubt anyone heard us. This place—"

There was an odd noise coming from ahead of them, a heavy rustling noise, and both boys froze.

"Uh-oh."

"*Grrrooooowwwlllp?*"

The door at the end of the hallway slowly opened, and something poked its way through.

A giant bird, was Gerard's first thought. But

what was a bird doing in there? Then more of the body came through—a long, pelted, sinewy neck, coated in a thick shag of hair, followed by massive paws and shoulders.

"By all that's holy!" Newt yelped. "A griffin!"

Trust Newt to recognize a creature, no matter how magical.

"Should we run?" Gerard asked.

"Where?" Newt replied, staring in delighted fascination at the creature coming toward them in an oddly cat-like, belly-to-the-ground crawl. "Back down the hall? It will be on us in an instant. Into one of the rooms? And wait there for how long?"

"So we sit and get eaten here?"

"Pity you lost your sword during our swim, isn't it?" Newt sounded oddly calm for someone about to be eaten alive.

Gerard took some comfort from that. Newt was generally pretty much against being eaten, or otherwise made dead.

"Grrrllll?"

"Hello there," Newt said, staying perfectly still.

"Is it . . . like the dragon? Is it intelligent?"

"About the same level as a dog," Newt said, then paused. "At least, I think."

"You think?" Gerard responded in a harsh whisper. "You *think*?"

"I've never actually seen one before. Just heard stories. I think . . . I think this one's still a kitten."

Since the kitten was the size of a large horse, Gerard did not feel at all relieved by that news.

"And what do we do if momma's still around?"

"Not much," Newt said. "Hey, boy. Hey there. Aren't you a good boy, yes you are."

He was keeping his voice even, conversational, and the griffin seemed to be responding well, rising up off his belly a little and tracking him with his gaze.

But maybe, Gerard thought uneasily, he was just getting ready to spring.

"*Grrrlll?*"

"That's an odd meow," Gerard said, then reconsidered. How else could a bird-headed cat meow, except oddly?

"I . . ." Newt seemed suddenly hesitant. "I don't think he's meowing, exactly."

"Exactly?"

"Ailis," Newt said.

Gerard looked around to see who Newt was speaking to, then his head swung back around like it was on a swivel when the creature responded: *"Grrrrll?"*

"Yes, girl," Newt said. "Can you take us to the girl?"

The griffin seemed to consider that for a moment, then turned in the narrow space, and headed back out the door he came in through, turning his head back once as though to say, "Well? After all that, aren't you coming?"

"Holy . . ." Gerard breathed deeply, but followed Newt when he went after the griffin down the hall and through a pair of swinging doors.

* * *

"Sir Tawny! Where have you been?" Ailis's voice was coming from a room down the hallway. The griffin bounded forward, still uttering its plaintive call. The boys exchanged glances and hurried after, impatient to get to Ailis and get out of this place. It had taken them seemingly forever to reach this hallway, and yet it was just a hallway down from the hallway they had started in. Or so it seemed.

"Magic," Newt had muttered more than once. "I'm trapped in an entire building made of magic."

They caught up with the griffin outside a door.

Clearly it was unable to go into the room itself, but stuck its head in to receive scratches on its head. Unfortunately, that meant that there was no way for Newt or Gerard to enter, or be seen by anyone inside the room.

"Ailis?"

"Gerard?" There was total, absolute astonishment in her voice, and then a *"mrowr"* of protest from Sir Tawny as he was eased back out into the hallway.

The three of them stared at each other for a moment, then Ailis was hugging them both, hard, and babbling about how she didn't think anyone knew where she was, how did they know where she was, how did they find her?

"I saw Morgain steal you," Gerard finally managed to say. "Merlin sent us here. And 'Sir Tawny' led us to you. We've come to take you home."

Ailis blinked at them, one hand reaching out to scratch again at Sir Tawny's feathers as he snuck his head back in through the doorway. "Home? But . . . I'm not ready to go."

Silence fell on the room. Even Sir Tawny seemed taken aback by her words.

"What? Ailis, are you . . . Morgain! She's enspelled you!"

"She has not! Newt, you don't understand!"

Newt glared at her, hands fisted at his hips. "You're right. I don't."

"I didn't ask to be taken, and I didn't ask to be rescued, and I didn't ask to be treated like a piece of property by anyone who thinks that they know what's best for me!" She paused to gasp for breath, pushing hair off her face as though trying to cool down.

"You don't know what you're saying," Gerard started, then immediately realized that was the wrong thing to say, even before she turned on him.

"How do you know what I know? You don't know *anything*. You haven't . . . you and *your* life and *your* plans and *your* goals—well, maybe I have some, too, now!"

Gerard opened his mouth to retort. Instead, he waited for a rise of warmth to come and give him wisdom, or cunning. But the spell-touch was silent. Neither Merlin nor Arthur had much luck with women either, apparently.

"And you'll reach them here, these goals?" Newt asked. His voice was calmer than theirs, slipping into the tone he used to calm aggressive dogs. People responded to it almost as well, and Ailis was no exception.

"I don't know. But what chance do I have in Camelot? They'll just put me back in the solar and think that they are doing me a favor."

"But aren't they—" Gerard began, then paused when all three—Ailis, Newt, and Sir Tawny—turned to stare at him.

"What do you want, then?" Newt asked. "Power?"

She grimaced, then shook her head. "Not the way you mean it, Newt. I know what you're saying and—no. I don't want that sort of power. Not like Morgain. Not even like Merlin. Just . . . to be able to control my own life. To decide what I do and where I go."

"Ailis, nobody has that kind of power. Not even Arthur."

"Morgain does."

Gerard couldn't stand it anymore. "Is that why she was in Camelot, spying on Arthur? Ailis, she's evil!"

"So everyone keeps telling me. But they can't tell me *why*. So I guess 'evil' all depends on your definition of the word, doesn't it? I'm not saying I don't want to go home ever," she went on, walking to the sofa. She sat down and continued, "Just . . . not yet.

And when I do, it will be as I decide." She smiled at them as she said that, a sweet smile that did nothing to undercut the bitterness of her words.

"All right, then," Gerard said, surprising them all. "You'll stay. And we'll stay with you. Until you decide that you're ready to leave." What he was saying sounded insane. He knew that. But in the face of Ailis's unexpected stubbornness, what was Gerard supposed to do? Throw her over his shoulder and carry her, kicking and screaming, off the island? He didn't need Merlin's cunning or Arthur's wisdom to know that wouldn't work. And it gave them a reason to stay, to look around. Odds were, Ailis wasn't going to share anything she might have learned of Morgain's plans, either, the way her thoughts were all tangled up.

I won't fail you, the way I failed Ailis, he thought, although he wasn't sure if the words were directed to Arthur, Merlin, or Sir Caedor.

A gentle voice interjected. "It is generally considered polite to ask your hostess if you are even welcome to stay, before deciding upon such a thing."

All three jumped as Morgain strolled into the room, elegantly dressed in a gown of dark blue. Her expression was cool, distant, and somewhat amused.

Newt looked horrified, Gerard looked cautiously nervous, and Ailis looked guilty.

"Morgain, I . . . I invited them. I—"

"Witch-child." Morgain lost some of her amusement. "Never lie to me."

Ailis bowed her head. Gerard suddenly noted that her auburn hair was unbraided. He hadn't seen her hair out of its normal thick braids falling over her face since they were children. And was that a feather knotted into the red strands?

"Yes, Morgain. I am sorry. But you won't make them leave, will you?"

The sorceress sighed. "I did let them enter my home. Yes, of course I knew you boys were here. What good is it being me, if I cannot tell who is inside my very own walls? I let them enter, nonetheless, knowing that they were brought here only by their concern for you. Is that fact—the fact that they not only live, but were allowed to find you—reassurance enough?"

Ailis still felt guilty, but a stubborn glint was in her eyes when she looked up. "No. I want your word that they'll be safe here."

Morgain let out an undignified snort of laughter, and for a moment she looked barely five years older than Ailis herself.

Ailis could almost see Morgain's brain working. After even this short time, she was beginning to understand how her teacher thought. Were the boys enemies? Or potentially useful allies?

She had let them into her fortress, so she did not fear them. But Morgain was nothing if not complicated, and she surely had hidden reasons for what she did. What was important was that she not reject them out of hand. Because if Morgain thought they were a threat, spies sent to report back to Camelot on her plans, that would be altogether different.

"Gerard and I have been friends for a long time. He was concerned about me. Now that he knows I am content, there is no cause for alarm. Right?"

She focused intently in Gerard's direction, willing him to pick up on her cue. To her surprise, however, it was Newt who responded.

"It does seem as though we came all this way to rescue a fair maiden who needs no rescuing," he said with a laugh that sounded too forced for Ailis's comfort.

"I'm sorry that you came all this way for nothing," she responded, still wishing Gerard would stop standing there like a lump and join in—to show that he understood that there was no need to confront

Morgain. If he would just play along, Morgain would not hurt them.

"Done and done. If they are that dear to you, and you to them, then of course the boys may stay as long as you wish them to." The sorceress paused, her expression growing stern again. "And not a moment longer."

"Thank you, Morgain." Ailis heard what the boys might not have, that the option was not to let them go, but to kill them. Ailis was the valued pawn here, not them.

"And you are not to allow them to interfere with your studies." The threat in Morgain's voice was clear this time. So long as Ailis remained obedient, the boys would be well-treated. "If they must practice their weapon skills, I will have a teacher come in." She cast a thoughtful glance at Gerard, clearly remembering the fact that he had managed to defeat her in armed combat the last time. "In fact, I think I will insist upon it. The witch-child's is not the only talent I cannot bear to see wasted by the closed minds of Camelot."

"Even knowing that I might eventually use those skills against you, Lady Morgain?" Gerard asked. Ailis drew a sharp breath of alarm.

The sorceress laughed. "Even so, young squire. Who knows? Like my young apprentice here, you may begin to understand more of the world around you, see that there is more to it than Camelot, and Arthur-says-so, or Merlin-says-so."

Gerard was feeling a little like he had the first time he was knocked off his horse during a tourney practice. The world was spinning slightly askew. He knew something was going on around him, but he couldn't quite focus on it. This all seemed very . . . wrong. He knew it was wrong, that he wasn't supposed to be agreeing to all this. But it also seemed practical and reasonable. Ailis was safe and healthy. Morgain was agreeing, in effect, to a truce while Ailis made up her mind. It wasn't as though there was anything back at Camelot for them to rush back to, either.

Or was there?

The Quest. Right. And they were here for a reason. Information. They were supposed to be gathering information—to find out what Morgain was planning, why she seemed so dead-set against Arthur's Quest. He remembered that now.

Somehow, though, seeing Ailis's smile, and Newt's fascination with the griffin . . . and yes, he admitted it, the thought of learning some of the moves, perhaps, that Morgain had used when they fought, sword-strokes different from any he and the other squires were being taught back home, was appealing.

This was dangerous, consorting with the enemy. Justification after justification slid through his mind. He could stay. Win Morgain's trust. Win Ailis back to them. If he could come back with information useful to Arthur, useful to Merlin, they would overlook other things. Hadn't Arthur himself decreed that Morgain was not to be killed, because of the shared blood that ran in their veins? Perhaps he could even convince Morgain that it was time to put away her anger, and join her brother's Court!

Visions of glory raced through his head. Perhaps he could become the youngest squire to ever be knighted. He could eventually earn himself a seat at the Round Table!

That was all he had ever wanted, all he had ever worked for. And if staying here, with Morgain, for a little while, could earn him that . . .

Some small voice in the back of his head was still protesting. This was wrong. This was some glamour, some magic of Morgain's twisting his thoughts, confusing him. There was more here that they were supposed to be doing, something that needed to be done *now*. . . . Gerard shut that voice out. He was here for Ailis. Ailis was safe. He would bring Ailis home, just a little later than they had planned.

"Enough!"

All four humans jumped at the sound of the new voice. Sir Tawny reacted to the intrusion by posturing for an attack, and ended up stuck halfway in and halfway out of the doorway. His head slammed against the doorjamb and made him let out a yowl of pain that simply added to the clamor and confusion.

Tall, was all Gerard could think. *Towering,* although the figure in front of them could not have been much more than Morgain's own height— certainly nowhere near as tall or broad as most of the knights of Camelot. But the heavy gray hooded cape gave an ominous air to the newcomer, an impression only aided by the way Ailis cringed away from it.

"How dare you enter here?" Morgain asked the shadow-figure, standing, almost instinctively, between Ailis and it.

"I dare because you have called it upon yourself, Morgain Le Fay. Or have you forgotten all, in the midst of this foolishness? You brought me here. You fed me. You gave me entry into their lives. And now you waste your time and magic attempting to win over these . . . playthings.

"There is no more time for distractions. You have wasted enough time with that child, much less allowing two more to clutter the path."

Gerard felt for where his sword should have been, wishing more than anything for his fingers to close around the comforting coolness of its hilt, to feel the weight of the blade in his hand. Not that it would do him any good. The thing in front of them spoke in a voice like thunder and radiated heat like a white-burning fire. Gerard knew as well as he knew his own name that nothing that looked or sounded like that was going to fall under a simple metal sword.

It was up to Morgain to protect them—or not.

The hooded figure spoke again. "You have important things to do, Morgain Le Fay. Are you still committed to this? Are you still willing to sacrifice for this?"

Morgain stood tall and proud for a long moment, then her shoulders slumped slightly. Her head dipped in acknowledgment of these words.

"Get rid of them," the figure commanded. "Then

come to me. The world turns, and our time has come to act. It is your moment of glory, Morgain. Do not let it pass."

The figure pivoted and left the room without another word. Morgain turned a gaze gone cold as ice upon them.

TWENTY

The three were quickly taken prisoner by ghostly servants summoned by the imperious snap of Morgain's fingers. Ailis was allowed to bundle up some of her belongings, but Newt and Gerard were not to help her. Morgain, meanwhile, stood in the middle of the room and watched everything with a cold, distant expression.

When Ailis indicated she had everything she wanted—a book, a small blanket, and a few trinkets—Morgain led the way down the hallway to where they were to be kept until their fate was decided. Morgain's back was straight and her shoulders squared under her gown, but Newt had the feeling that she was as much a prisoner as they were.

The figure had frightened Ailis and Gerard but Newt had felt a different chill. Not fear, but familiarity. There was something about the being that ticked in the back of his mind, back in a place and a time he never thought about anymore.

He didn't want to think about it now, either. So he focused instead on the sights and sounds around him; how the servants accompanying them made no noise when they walked, the way the long feather in Ailis's hair flipped back and forth with her breathing, the fact that they had been walking far longer now than could be justified by the length of the corridor as seen from the outside, and that he could sense the soft padding noises of something following them.

Morgain finally stopped in front of a door and opened it with a twitch of her fingers.

"Inside."

The room was about the size of Ailis's sitting room, but it was unfurnished, with no windows or fireplace.

"Food will be brought," Morgain said. "I am unfamiliar with the appetites of boys your age. If you are still hungry, Ailis will show you how to call for more."

Thanking her seemed out of place, considering their circumstances, so all three remained silent. Morgain didn't seem to notice.

"I must go. Stay out of sight and keep out of trouble, and you may yet live through this night." The servants filtered out of the room, and the sorceress followed, pausing only to allow a low-flowing shape to pass by her into the room. With black fur and golden-green eyes, Newt recognized the cat that had been with Morgain back on the Isle of Apples.

"She will guard you," Morgain said, and shut the door firmly behind herself, leaving the three alone. A solid click of the door being locked echoed into the silence.

"Guard us? Great." Newt looked nervously at the cat, who stared back at him in a manner quite unlike most large cats he had ever encountered. The beast seemed to be amused by his nervousness.

Gerard, meanwhile, had focused on something else entirely. "What did she mean, 'stay out of sight'? What else are we likely to do while locked in here?"

Ailis sat down on the floor and folded the fabric of her skirt to the side of her to make a cushion of sorts. She then patted the makeshift nest. The boys watched in amazement as the cat crawled over and curled up with its head resting on her knee.

"Some guard," Newt said.

"Oh, she's fierce. I've seen her take down a deer

in flight," Ailis said casually, as though there was unlimited space for a deer to roam these halls. Then again, there probably was. There could have been an entire herd of them around the next corner.

"You're calm about all of this," Gerard observed, "considering Morgain just pretty much betrayed you."

"Betrayed?" Ailis looked up, honestly surprised. "There was no betrayal. Not by Morgain's standards, anyway."

"She promised—"

"She promised to teach me, to not send you away without my consent, to allow us to remain unscathed. Has she broken any of those promises?"

Gerard threw up his hands in exasperation. "She's locked us up. And I don't think it's so she can deliver us back to the safety of Camelot at her convenience."

"She hates Camelot," Ailis agreed. "And I know now why."

When the boys stared at her, she shrugged. "Merlin helped cause her father's death. He manipulated her mother, all for the sole purpose of creating Arthur. Once there was a male heir, Morgain wasn't important anymore, not the way she was raised to be. Wouldn't that make you bitter?"

"A male child—" Gerard started, protesting.

"That's not always the way it's been," Newt said thoughtfully. "In some lines, the female child was the one who inherited. Still is that way, in some places."

"Not here." Gerard was confident in that.

"Not in Arthur's Britain, no." Ailis sounded bitter herself. "But Morgain's family remembers before, when the Romans came. They were here when Boadiccia was queen."

"Who?"

Newt sighed, as though not believing Gerard could be that ignorant. "Boadiccia. Queen of the Icini. The Romans invaded and tried to take power from her family. She rebelled and was killed." When everyone—including the cat—looked at Newt, he shrugged. "People talk about a lot of things in the stable that they don't mention in Arthur's halls."

"So, Morgain believes that she has cause to be angry with Merlin and Arthur." Gerard was adding things up in his head. "Is that why she's so set against us winning the Grail? Because it will make Arthur's hold on the throne that much more powerful?"

Ailis reached over and petted the cat until it relaxed back to her knee. "I think so. She wants it for herself, too, but mostly it's to strike against Arthur.

To make him too weak to hold the throne, so that he's not Arthur the High King, anymore."

"And what's going on now?" Newt asked. "Is it related to the Quest? Is that what that . . . person meant about it being time to act?" Surely by now, the Quest should have already departed, each knight racing to be the one to find the prize and bring it home.

"I don't know." Ailis shrugged. "That . . . person hasn't been happy that I am here. I know they're planning something, some way to destroy the Quest, something that it thinks I'm distracting Morgain from accomplishing."

"How?"

"I don't know. It wasn't like I was stopping her from doing anything—not like I *could* have stopped her." Ailis reached up to stroke the feather in her hair absentmindedly. "I hope Morgain's all right."

"What?" Gerard's exclamation was loud enough to rouse the cat again, who half-opened its slitted eyes and glared at him.

"I said I hope that she's all right. This stranger has her worried. I can tell."

"Maybe she should be worried," Newt said. "You need to be careful who you invite into your home. Sometimes, they don't leave so easily."

"We should be more worried about how *we're* going to leave," Gerard said.

"Leaving really isn't a problem," Ailis said offhandedly.

"Right," Newt said. "Ailis, you know I care for you, but I think that your brains have softened, sitting here, inside this . . . place."

She pushed the cat gently off her knee and stood up. "You doubt me?" Her tone was imperious, offended. She walked over to the door, which they had all heard Morgain lock, and placed her palm flat against the wood. "Walls are for keeping. Doors are for leaving. If I choose, I leave."

There was an audible click, and the door swung open into the hallway.

"It's not that difficult," Ailis said. "Morgain knew such a simple spell wouldn't keep us locked up. That's what her words meant."

"Come on, cat." And with that, she walked out into the hall, the great black cat close on her heels.

Newt and Gerard looked at each other, then at the now-empty doorway, and practically ran each other over, trying to be the next one out of their prison.

"You know the way out?" Newt asked, since

Ailis was walking with a determined stride that indicated she had a goal in mind.

"No. I need to find Morgain."

"Morgain? Ailis, have you lost your mind?" Gerard caught Ailis by the arm, then dropped it again when she turned on him, her eyes wide and angry. The cat snarled, low and dark, its ears flat against its skull.

"Right," Gerard said, taken aback. "Morgain."

Newt fell in beside Gerard as Ailis raced with disturbing certainty down the unmarked hallway. "Look on the bright side," he said quietly. "Maybe she'll send our bodies home when she gets over being annoyed."

"Shut up, Newt," Gerard said, mainly because he had been thinking exactly the same thing—and wasn't sure if the 'she' he was thinking of was Morgain, or Ailis.

TWENTY-ONE

Ailis led them up a short flight of stairs to a huge blackwood door that made both Gerard and Newt hang back, although neither of them could quite say why.

"Are you sure we should . . . I don't think we're supposed to go in there," Newt said.

Ailis had been certain of her actions walking up the stairs, but the last few steps her feet had slowed, like they were moving through something thick and sticky. Her face had gone from determined to puzzled. "I don't . . . understand."

"Maybe she's not so good a friend as you thought?" Gerard's voice was nastier than he meant it to be.

"She's not a friend," Ailis said. "She's my teacher." There was a difference clear in Ailis's mind.

Gerard and Newt, comforting behind her, and Sir Tawny, upset at being left behind—those were her friends. Morgain was no friend, but she wasn't an enemy either. Ailis was pretty sure of that.

"Well, maybe this is another lesson," Newt said. "Ailis, if we go in there . . ."

But Ailis had already reached the door and used that same wiggle-finger motion Morgain had used on other doors. It slid into the wall and she slipped inside.

Muttering something Newt couldn't quite hear, Gerard went in after her. Newt considered turning tail and going back the way they came, but even as he thought it, his feet were carrying him forward. They were in this together, no matter who was stupid enough to lead.

Newt entered the room, finding a large open workspace already holding four other people: Ailis, Gerard, Morgain, and the shadow-figure, standing in the center of the room. Above the table in front of him, a hammered metal bowl hung in midair, simmering over flames that seemed to come from nowhere, causing a thick, noxious, purple-colored fume to rise into the air.

"Get out!" Morgain turned to face them, her

expression savage, lips pulled back from her perfect teeth in a horrible snarl. "Get out of here!"

"Morgain!" Ailis cried, and was shoved away by a wave of the sorceress's hand. She staggered a few steps then regained her balance, glaring at her teacher with almost equal anger. "Morgain, no! Think about what you're doing!"

Whatever it was that Morgain was doing, Ailis was afraid of it. That was enough for Newt, who was getting ready to grab his friends and run like the hounds of the wild hunt were after them.

"I have thought. For *years* I've thought. And now the time has come to act."

Morgain turned back to the pot, holding her long-fingered hands over the smoke. "Let those who stand against me, in white-stoned towers, let those who stand against me, in Camelot's golden hour; let them come to this, in night's darkest moment: chaos, confusion, the white-foaming madness!"

Ailis let out a sob as Morgain dropped a pinch of some other substance into the foul pot, and stirred it, then began her chant again.

"Let those who stand—"

"Lady Morgain," Gerard interrupted her, sounding as Gerard never had before, in the short time

Newt had known him. Even Ailis seemed taken aback by the timbre and forcefulness in his voice. "You conspire against your rightful king, ruler of these lands, and in doing so commit crimes for which you must be judged. For the sake of your ties to him, and the blood you two share, cease now, and he may yet again show you mercy."

The laughter that came from Morgain's mouth made the hair on the back of Newt's neck rise, and even Ailis blanched, as she had not when the words of the spell were first spoken.

"Little fool. Arthur has never once shown me mercy, never once shown me any regard at all, save for his own vanity and pride. King of all Britons? Not here. Not on these islands. Not over these people. They are mine. And they shall have what is theirs—and know *me* as their savior. You foiled me once, but this time, I shall succeed."

"It *is* the Grail that you seek," Gerard said. "But it is not yours for the taking, sorceress."

Her snarl widened. "It is already mine! It belongs to the Old Ways, not the new—a chalice of blood-infused power. I shall hold it and rededicate it, and with its power take back that which was stolen from me."

Newt could see Ailis taking Morgain's words in, like blows to her body, and his heart ached for her.

"Kill that boy-child, and be done with it," the figure ordered. It did not seem to consider Gerard a real threat, but Morgain was fixated on the squire's words.

"You see the Grail only as a means to an end, not for the glory of itself, its history. You don't understand what it means to the man who holds it." Gerard was working up an impressive temper himself.

"The *man* who holds it, little squire?" Morgain's voice was so sharp it could have harvested an entire field of wheat. "You make a great assumption, there. The Grail is power. That is all. Power is everything, for the world is split into those who have it, and those who do not. My people demand it of me. The chalice of legend, the cup of holy blood, will be their protection, and I will be their protector."

"Protect them against whom? Arthur is a fair king, a just leader and—"

"And a man." Ailis cut into Gerard's outrage with a clear, carrying voice. "He is only a man, a mortal, magic-less, and as such not suited to bear such a powerful object. The balance of power is delicate, and no warrior raised only to metal and fire can understand what must be done."

The shadow-figure hissed in displeasure at Ailis's insolence. Gerard looked at Ailis as though she had lost her senses entirely. But Morgain smiled at Ailis approvingly, some of her venom diluted. "Yes. Arthur is so dedicated to his way, his Cup of the Christ, he does not remember the Old Ways, the ways he was born into."

Gerard clearly had no idea what the two women were talking about, but Newt did. Most of the knights were Christians, or claimed no particular allegiance, and Merlin always kept his own thoughts to himself on such matters. Because of that, it was not often spoken out loud. But there were many within Camelot who looked to the Old Gods; the trinity of Mother, Maiden, and Crone as opposed to Father, Son, and Holy Spirit; the warrior-goddess Athena, the death-gatherer Ankou, or others, unnamed and half-forgotten with the influx of the followers of Christ.

Newt didn't bow to any gods, not local, not Roman, not from far-off lands he had never seen. But that didn't mean he didn't believe they existed. And far too many were being invoked in this room for his comfort.

He touched the band on his arm and acknowledged the humor of finding comfort in a purely human-given gift when facing dire magics.

"Arthur might learn, if he were given the right guidance," Ailis said, her feet taking her in small, slow steps closer to Morgain, almost as though she didn't know she was moving. "If someone who was loved by the Goddess, versed in the Old Ways, were to have access to his mind, and his heart. . . "

"Ailis, don't be a fool . . ." Gerard hissed.

"They took him from me," Morgain said, her anger sparking again. "Merlin took him from me when Arthur was but a babe. And raised him as his own, he who had no right to a child!"

"Then should you not take him back? And restore him to the Old Ways?" Ailis suggested.

Gerard started to protest, about to draw further attention to himself. Newt gave in to the urge to kick the squire, hard, in the shin. When Gerard turned to glare at him, Newt returned the look with his best "shut up, then" expression, hoping that his friend was smart enough to figure out that Ailis knew what she was doing. She was the negotiator, the one who had kept them from being killed on their first journey. And, more to the point, magic was inside her, the way it was inside Morgain. No matter how Newt himself might distrust magic, right now it might be their only chance to survive.

"It is too late for that, witch-child," Morgain responded, turning back to the potion. "Arthur is a grown man now. He has shown he cannot be persuaded, nor turned from his path." Her voice sounded almost as though she were smiling on the inside. "He is as stubborn as all the rest of our family, in truth." The levity disappeared. "And for that stubbornness, as the rest of us have suffered, so must he."

Ailis nodded slowly, as though agreeing with Morgain, even as she reached the woman's side, one hand rising as though to take her teacher's hand in her own.

"Morgain . . ." the shadow-figure warned.

Newt shifted and dropped the silver band, intentionally distracting the shadow-figure, even though it made his skin crawl to do so. The thing tracked him with a malevolent gaze, hatred seething so furiously that Newt could practically feel it. What had he ever done to this being? Why did it seem to hate him and Ailis so much, but not Gerard? Whatever the reason, his trick was working. The figure was paying attention to him, and Ailis was almost to the worktable.

Whatever you're planning to do, Ailis, he thought, *do it fast!*

"Ailis," Gerard said, his voice pleading. "Why are you doing this? Why are you siding with them?"

"Maybe because you're wrong, Ger. Maybe because you've always been wrong." She shot him a glance filled with scorn, then turned back to the table and her teacher.

Ailis reached out to investigate the contents of the steaming bowl. Before Morgain could slap her hand away, as she clearly meant to do, Ailis had taken a handful of the smoke and clenched it into her palm, chanting frantically: "Isolate, inviolate, insulate; protect the blood, all the blood, from harm willful or missent."

"Nooooooo!" the shadow-figure roared, lunging for Ailis, the noise rising and filling the entire room until Newt thought his ears would bleed, his head explode. He felt the floor rushing up to meet him in a distinctly unpleasant manner.

I hate *magic,* was all he could think.

TWENTY-TWO

"**W**itch-child, no!"

Morgain's cry was overridden by the shadow-figure's outburst, but Ailis heard her nonetheless. She reached for the anguish in that voice instinctively, trying to ease her teacher's concern even as the magical counterattack knocked her backward, off her feet, and slammed her into the wall.

"Get away from her, Le Fay. This has gone on too long. The threads are tangled, the future misdirected, and she is to blame."

"You may not have her. Not her. She is the only daughter I will ever know." That was Morgain, standing between Ailis and that awful, horrible, terrifying slithery whisper of a voice. Ailis wondered if she was dead—if they were all dead, and this was hell, and that the devil had come to claim them.

"I have everyone in the end, Le Fay. Even her. Even you."

Ailis was trying to track their exchange, but almost all of her concentration was focused on the tiny bit of power she still held in her palm. It had been a simple spell, one she had cobbled together as best she could in the moment between realization and action. Born out of equal parts of compassion for Morgain, and fear of what the sorceress might do in her pain and anger, the spell was not a defensive one, but reflexive. It did not strike out against anyone or anything, but deflected the aggressive spell; made it impotent.

Ailis didn't know how she knew all this. It was as though the knowledge had risen up through the stones, the same way she had known the figure in robes was no friend to her from the instant it walked into the room. *Why* had Morgain allowed it onto her island? What had it promised her, cajoled her with?

Evil was all in how you looked at it. Morgain had reasons for everything she did. Merlin had reasons. Arthur had reasons. Everyone had reasons.

No matter the reasons, now. What was important now was the spell she held—that she keep it hidden, keep it safe.

Even as she thought that, the shadow-figure

raised its arm to make another strike against her. Power gathered, thickening the air until Ailis could barely breathe.

On the floor, Gerard stirred, his hand reaching out to find something, anything, he could use as a weapon. It was useless. There was no way he could stop the shadow-figure. No way any of them could.

The shadow-figure tightened its fingers into a fist, rising to come down on Ailis.

"Morgain . . ." If only to her own ears, the name sounded painfully like "mother," and Ailis flinched more from that than the attack about to come. She risked a glance up at the figure's face, and saw Morgain already in motion, not toward Ailis, but away from her, directly into the path of the shadow-figure's blow.

"No!" the sorceress cried, and the two adults disappeared in a shower of silver-black sparks that hit Ailis like a storm-wracked wave, lit the entire room into painful clarity, then plunged it into complete darkness as they faded.

* * *

Morgain?
Silence.

Merlin?

More silence.

"Ailis?"

In the darkness, she could hear Newt's voice, reassuringly solid and familiar, then the sound of bodies shifting, picking themselves up off the floor. She lay where she was, feeling aches in every part of her body, but she focused on the tiny glow still intact and still in her hand.

"Are you all right?" Newt, his hands gentle and comforting on her shoulder, urged her to respond.

"I think so," she told him. "Help me up."

It took both boys to get Ailis to a standing position. Where they had merely been knocked to the ground by the shadow-figure's last attack, she had been literally blasted by its magic. Once on her feet, although unsteady, Ailis opened her palm and let the spell-light glow more strongly, lighting her way to the worktable.

"So . . . tired."

"Draw on me." Newt, still supporting her, whispered in her ear. "Draw on us both. You know how. Don't think—do. Do what you need to do."

He was right. The knowledge rose from deep within her. She felt strength flow from where their skin met hers, giving her the ability to focus on the task at hand.

The pot still simmered. It was still a threat, however abandoned and contained. Ailis raised her palm over the smoke. Flinching a little from the fumes, she concentrated, and sent the spell back down into the green liquid. The scrap of fumes she had originally stolen met and merged with the source, taking with it the spell she had created.

"It is like cooking," Morgain had said. Sometimes, adding a single spice changed the entire complexion of the dish. Sometimes, you had to improvise.

"It's safe now. I think." Morgain had only shown her the basics of spell-making; everything else she had guessed at. All she could do was her best, and hope Merlin would be able to protect them against anything else.

Merlin.

Merlin?

Child? Ailis?

She caught at that distant voice, anchored herself, then raised her eyes to the far wall where a faint glimmer was forming.

Ropes, under her fingers. Pulleys. Open here, close there, send one way and not the other . . .

"What is that?" Newt asked, not having seen the transport portal before.

"A way home," Ailis said, even as Gerard instinctively averted his eyes, anticipating the blast of light that had occurred back in Camelot. She reached out a hand, her fingers flexing and stretching as though manipulating something the others could not see. "Come on."

"Are you sure? Did you make that? Or was it . . ." and Newt scanned around as though expecting Morgain to pop out at them again.

"Look!" Gerard said, pointing. Through the green glow, all three could see the familiar stone corridors of Camelot, the leg of a chair, and . . . yes, glimpses of Merlin's robes, as he floated back and forth!

"Hurry," Ailis said as the vision shimmered. "It won't last long. We have to go!"

TWENTY-THREE

"Gahhhh!" Merlin glared at the three of them, then carefully pried himself off the ceiling, and lowered himself slowly back down to the floor. He took a moment to brush himself off and adjust his robes. Then and only then did he look up to meet their carefully straight-faced expressions.

"So nice of you to come by to see me, however unexpectedly. Ailis, child, it's good to see you." Merlin looked at them carefully, and didn't ask where Sir Caedor was, or what had happened to their horses or supplies. Or how they had managed to suddenly appear in the middle of his private rooms.

"You've been away for some time," was all he said. "Arthur's been gone and back with his Marcher Lords already. I was beginning to become somewhat worried."

"The Quest?" Gerard asked, focusing on the thing that had been all-important to him not so long ago.

"Is about to ride out, if not the next morning, then the day after that. They have been waiting only for better weather—something stirred up a nasty storm in the north, and we've been feeling the effects of it even down here. But come, sit, tell me everything. Ailis, you fairly glow of magic. What *have* you been up to?"

She opened up her hand, where a trace of her spell still lingered. "Morgain wants the Grail," she started. "For her own glory, but also because she believes that it's the only way to protect her beliefs, her way of life, against Arthur. Something about the land, the Old Ways . . . I didn't quite understand all of it. But she believes, passionately."

Merlin nodded, as though none of this was really a surprise to him. "Her family is too rooted," he said. "Old trees are strong, but they don't stand forever."

"She has players on the field," Ailis continued. "She's trying to match them to yours, as best I could tell. But I'm not sure what she's going to do with them. I don't think she knows, exactly. That was why she was in the castle, to learn what our plans were. Only . . .

"There was another . . . person there in her fortress. Someone with a lot of power, helping her . . ."

Merlin suddenly looked alert. "Go on, child."

Ailis told the rest of her story. Newt and Gerard were practically squirming in their seats with the desire to interrupt with their own take on events.

"And then Morgain . . . they both disappeared. I think maybe she saved us." Ailis ended. She reached up to touch the feather in her hair as though seeking reassurance from it. Then she used that same hand to reach out and touch Newt, sitting beside her. He tried to smile and closed his own hand over hers, warm and human and comforting.

"This shadow-figure Ailis described . . . have you anything more to add?" Merlin finally asked the boys.

Gerard shook his head. "It was almost as though I couldn't look directly at it. Him. Her. I don't even know what it was. Its voice . . . the voice scared me. It was like a cold knife at the base of your neck."

Newt started to say something, then merely nodded his agreement. Anything else he thought of was just from myths, stories from his childhood, things that had no place here in this room.

The enchanter looked carefully at all three of them, each in turn. "All right. There are things the three of you aren't telling me, but I'll trust your judgment that Arthur and I don't need to know whatever it is. And that if you change your minds, you'll come to me."

Merlin sat back and looked at them as a whole, contemplating, until all three were squirming in their seats again.

"It's good that you're back now. You need to travel with the Quest. All three of you, not just master squire here."

Newt looked astonished, while Ailis almost fell off her stool in shock. "How?" she asked.

Newt, more pragmatic, asked, "Why?"

"I'll arrange it," Merlin said in a way that was not reassuring at all. "And because I suspect that it's important that you be there, whatever happens. You've been marked by this, the three of you. You've earned your place, and none may say otherwise. Not merely by being in the right place, but by being the right people in the right place, and not merely once, but twice now. Once is accident. Twice is fate. Three times . . ." Merlin looked at the three of them, his eyes tired and yet filled with a deep, luminous magic.

"Three times becomes legend."

And with that cryptic comment, he shooed the boys out of his study, commanding them to get some rest and let him handle everything for now. "Ailis, not you. The king wants to ask you a few questions further, if you don't mind. . . ."

The last view they had of Ailis was as Merlin propelled her away from them, by means of one firm hand on her shoulder, down the hall in the opposite direction.

*　*　*

There was no way—after all that—that sleep would be possible. Without discussion, the two remaining travelers found themselves sitting in the barn, in a stall that was currently without an equine occupant. The stable had the added advantage of being out of the way of the chaos that once again seemed to be gripping Camelot.

"You didn't say anything to Merlin about . . . about what happened," Gerard said. "About agreeing to stay with Morgain, in the fortress."

"Neither did you." Newt poked at the straw with one finger, idly.

"No, I didn't. It didn't . . . it didn't seem real,

everything that happened there. It doesn't seem real now—like that was all a dream. Everything up until then? Real. Sir Caedor's death. Real. The boat was far too real. But the moment we got to the fortress . . . it was like dream-time." Gerard turned to Newt. "What do you think?"

"It was real. It was all real."

"Of course it was. I meant—"

"I know what you meant. And it all felt real to me. Every minute." He paused. "Be thankful, if it's blurred for you."

"Yeah." Gerard shoved the straw with his foot, then blurted out, "Something's bothering you."

"Me?" Newt looked up, an innocent expression coming over his face.

"Yes, you. Something more than the fact that we've got to ride out tomorrow morning with half a dozen knights who're probably more like Sir Caedor than we would choose."

"You're getting smarter," Newt said, dropping the "dumb stable-boy" expression.

"You're getting more evasive. Is it still about all the magic stuff?"

Newt sighed, resigned to finally having this conversation. "A little. Not the magic itself, but . . ."

"You might as well tell me. Ailis can attest to the fact that I can be really stubborn once I start digging at something."

"It's not magic. It's what magic does to people." The words came out of his mouth as though they were being pulled from him, one letter at a time. "When I was a little kid . . . Ger . . . we have to watch Ailis."

"Watch her? Why? You think that Morgain might try something again?"

"I think . . . I think we keep getting away too easily. That portal we used to get back from the Orkneys—Ailis says she made it. But how? She says she can't do it now. Something in the fortress spoke to her, showed her how . . . but what if it actually was Morgain? Or, worse yet, the shadow-figure? What if they sent us back here and let Ailis think she did it on her own?"

"Why would they do that?"

"Why did Morgain agree to let us stay? Why did she take Ailis in the first place? It's all a long, convoluted plot to Morgain, you know that. Everything she does, it's all aimed at striking back at Arthur—the way we all wanted to stay there, even after just a few minutes? Think about it, Ger! Ailis was there so long, and was so enamored of that woman, and what she could do—" He stopped cold, and stared at his friend with a sudden thought. "Ger, what if Morgain didn't come to the castle to spy on Arthur at all? What if the goal was Ailis all along?"

"That's impossible. How? And why would Morgain care about one girl, even if she does have some magic? Ailis wouldn't ever endanger any of us."

"She might not be aware of it. She might not even be . . . Argh. I don't know." Newt put his head down in his hands, covering his face and shuddering like a horse shaking off flies.

Gerard was starting to follow the threads of Newt's thoughts, and he didn't like them at all. "You think they did something to her?"

"I think—I *know* that magic is addictive—appealing. We both felt that. Morgain . . . she can twist your mind. I know that I'd feel better if Merlin was keeping a close eye on Ailis, instead of sending her away."

"He's not sending her away. You heard him, we earned this spot, all three of us. Together."

When he saw that Newt still wasn't convinced, he went on. "We'll take care of her. Think about it, Newt. What better place to send someone who might be magic than into the company of half a dozen hardheaded knights who don't use magic—don't have any interest in magic—with her two best friends who know what to look for?"

Newt kept his face in his hands, but his shoulders relaxed a notch.

"We'll keep her safe, Newt. No matter what. That's what we did in the fortress. That's why Merlin's sending her with us. So we can keep her safe.

"And who knows," he said, suddenly thinking of it. "Maybe her magic, whatever it is, will help us find the Grail!"

They looked at each other, the same thought suddenly in their minds.

Newt spoke it for both of them. "And then Morgain—and the shadow-figure—will know where it is. Even if she wanted Ailis this go-around, more than any strike at Arthur, she was dead-serious about the Grail and what it meant to her. And we have no idea what it really means to the shadow-figure. Merlin has to—"

"Merlin has thought of it already."

Neither boy had heard the enchanter join them, and they jumped guiltily as he spoke, stammering their apologies.

"Enough already. If you're going to be fools enough to think I didn't know something like this was happening . . . had happened . . . was going to happen, then you think I'm even more of a doddering old fool than I actually am."

"Then why?" Gerard asked.

"Because it might not have. It still may not have. Ailis is a good girl, a wise girl, with a smart head on her shoulders and brave and loyal friends at her side. I did not lie—she has earned her place on this fool Quest, despite her gender. Were there not women who followed the Christ when he bled into this cup? Who is to say a woman is not the one to find it? In that, Morgain may be entirely correct."

"You want to use her, too. To find the Grail." Newt's tone was more of an accusation than was safe, speaking to an enchanter, but Merlin ignored it.

"Once we have the Grail, we will be in a better position to protect her—and any others who may be like her—from Morgain's reach. Camelot is safe. Ailis is safe. Arthur's kingship is safe. Everyone's happy, then," Merlin said.

If so, Newt wondered, why didn't any of them *look* particularly happy?

TWENTY-FOUR

"This," Gerard said in satisfaction. "Now *this* is how you're supposed to set off on a Quest!"

They were standing by their horses, waiting for the signal to mount. Around them, pennants snapped in the light breeze, and sunlight glimmered on the metal points of spears, catching highlights in the armor of the knights around them. Ailis was stroking the nose of the sturdy gelding she had been given. She was wearing trousers under her skirt, for easier riding astride, but her hair was tied up in her usual braid, the feather fastened to the end where it draped over her shoulder with a smaller version of the bands the boys wore on their arms. The queen had given it to her that morning, without ceremony, without words, but with a gentle hug and a kiss on the cheek for luck.

Ailis had to admit that Guinevere was quite sweet. No spine, no fire in her soul, but she took the beauty and the fortune that had been given to her and made the best of it. Ailis could see now that if you did the most with what you were given, you should feel no regret.

Ailis still didn't know what she had been given. She could see it in Gerard, how he stood a little taller, gave his opinion more clearly now. The death of Sir Caedor had dulled some of his shine, but tempered him at the same time, like a blade dipped in fire for the final proving before being taken into battle.

Newt, on the other hand, still seemed the same as ever. Deeper, maybe. He held himself more still, as though waiting for some sound only he would hear. She wondered what his change would be, then shook off that mood with an effort. *Let go of the past,* she could hear Merlin advising her. *Forget what Morgain taught you . . . for now. Wait. Grow stronger before you take too much onto yourself.*

"Looking forward to sleeping under a canopy?" she asked her friends, banishing thoughtfulness with teasing.

"Hah. Odds are, we'll be rolling our blankets under a tree somewhere, cursing the roots, same as always," Newt said. "Canopies are for knights and soft-skinned castle-dwellers."

"Certainly you're neither," Gerard said in return. "In fact, I think I heard someone saying they planned to use you for target practice, as your hide is so tough arrows will bounce right back to the archer."

"Funny."

Ailis leaned against her gelding, hearing it whiffle gently under her touch, and soaked in the strange normality of it all, the banter between her friends, the familiar sounds and smells of Camelot, even the bawling of a guardsman trying to maintain some sort of control over the chaos. The days spent with Morgain seemed so distant, now. Merlin had warned her about that; it wasn't magic, exactly, what had happened to her, but Morgain *had* been influencing her, trying to bring her over to the sorceress's side of things. *Don't rush into magic, no matter how appealing it may seem.*

Ailis had nodded when he said that, to show that she understood. It was Merlin who hadn't understood, though. She had known all along that Morgain was playing her. That didn't make what she learned any less true. It didn't make the fact that Morgain had protected her—*and* her friends—any less courageous.

It absolutely did not make her want to wait, to claim the strength she could now feel deep inside herself.

She reached up to touch the feather, smiling as she felt the familiar warmth of it in her fingers.

It didn't change the fact that she had felt the rise of something greater inside her. Something wonderful. Something magical. Something that was neither Merlin nor Morgain, but spoke directly to her. *Magic*. It was in her, too.

"You nervous?" Newt asked her, looking around at the insanity surrounding them.

"Terrified," she said, and smiled brilliantly at him until even his usual worried scowl relented, and he smiled back.

"Mount up!" came the call, and, anticipating the adventure to come, the three of them did.

**THE ADVENTURE CONTINUES
IN GRAIL QUEST BOOK 3:**

THE SHADOW
COMPANION

"Gather!"

The call came from the center of camp, and everyone turned to hear who was yelling.

"Gather!"

"That's Tom," Gerard said, relieved at the interruption. Tom was Sir Matthias's squire, the one who was actually stuck polishing gear and minding the horses. "Something must have happened. Come on!"

The two of them pushed through the crowd, slipping occasionally on the mud-slick grass, to where Sir Matthias was standing, a young, nervous-looking monk beside him. There were torches set up to hold the darkness at bay, but even with them, everything had a strange, shadowed cast that made Newt look around nervously, waiting for something to jump out at them.

"Nobody else feels it."

"What?"

Ailis had appeared next to Newt, looking straight ahead, watching not Sir Matthias but the monk with him. "The darkness. Nobody else can feel it."

"You do." Newt's words were less a statement than a question, most of his attention focused on making sure that she wasn't in any kind of physical distress.

"So do you. Feel it, I mean." That was a statement; they were sensing the same strange tension in the air, a tension which seemed to be increasing rather than fading.

Gerard had stopped listening to them, instead watching Sir Matthias and the monk like the rest of the crowd.

"Which means . . . ?" Newt wasn't sure what he was asking, whether it was about the darkness or the fact that they could feel it and nobody else could.

"I don't know," Ailis answered. "There's something about that man though. The monk. The darkness . . . it's strongest near him . . . it has been placed on him somehow, as though . . ."

"Shhhh," Gerard hushed them as Sir Matthias began to speak.

"This is Brother Jannot. He—"

"The Grail hides." The monk had a deep voice, deeper than his body should have been able to produce, and it carried even into the darkness. "The Grail hides in shadows, the long dark shadows. Bring the light, and dispel the shadows. Find the Grail."

"A prophecy," one of the knights muttered. "He's been gifted with the art of prophecy."

"A miracle," another said. "The voice of God speaks through him!"

Slowly, the mood of the gathered men changed from irritation and exhaustion to exultation, with Sir Matthias and the now-silent monk at the heart of it. Even Gerard and Newt got caught up in it, Newt totally forgetting his earlier unease.

Only Ailis, pushed to the side by the crowd trying to get close enough to touch the monk's robes, looked more distressed than uplifted by the prophecy.

"Something's wrong," she whispered, feeling it in her bones, in her blood. There was a sensation of the world being twisted somehow. She could feel it, taste it, in the monk's words. Magic was at work here, the kind of sinister magic she had felt once before. The Grail was in danger. They *all* were in danger.

"Something's wrong," she said again, a little louder this time.

But nobody heard her.

DEMCO